ONCE UPON A DARE

A RISKY BUSINESS NOVEL

JENNIFER BONDS

For my husband, Matt, whose unwavering support and endless patience has allowed me to make my dreams a reality.

1

OLIVIA

OLIVIA MASTERSON SURVEYED the Friday night clientele of Olive or Twist and came to the disturbing conclusion that she might be the only single twenty-something in the city of New York who wasn't ruled by her libido. Was she doing something wrong? It appeared she was the only one in the sleek bar not looking to get flat-out drunk tonight. Or laid. The proof was sitting right across the table from her in the form of her best friend Chloe, who was too busy checking out the competition to actually listen to a word she said.

Despite the swell of raging hormones, the atmosphere of the bar was relaxed with its dim lights, high top tables, and soft jazz music. That was one of the reasons she had chosen it. The other had to do with its proximity to the office, which was just down the block.

Truth be told, she'd rather be at home, curled up with a carton of Chicken Lo Mein and her Kindle, but Chloe had insisted they stop for a drink to celebrate Olivia's imminent promotion to partner at Pritchard & Associates, the advertising agency where they both worked. So here she was, spending her Friday night in a bar where the martinis were flowing and so were the pickup lines, and all she could think about was Chinese takeout.

Whatever that said about her, she wasn't going to dwell on it.

"Come on, Liv!" Chloe pouted, signaling the waitress for another round of drinks. "Loosen up already."

"If I didn't know better, I'd think you were trying to get me all liquored up and take advantage of the situation," Olivia teased, popping a blue cheese stuffed olive in her mouth.

Another perk of the martini bar—they had divine olives and weren't shy about dishing them out.

"You should be so lucky," Chloe countered, polishing off her drink with a rather unladylike gulp. "Considering the lack of actual sex in your sex life, I'd probably be the best you ever had."

"Hey..." Olivia's protest trailed off in a halfhearted sigh.

How could she argue with the logic? She hadn't had a man in her bed in, well, years.

It was a wonder she and Chloe had become such good friends

Chloe was a hopeless romantic desperately seeking Mr. Right, and Olivia spent most of her free time holed up in the office working on pitches. Not exactly glamorous, but it was a sacrifice she was willing to make.

Determined to make partner before her thirtieth birthday, she had made a lot of sacrifices in order to prove her father, and everyone else who doubted her abilities, wrong.

She'd had plenty of motivation along the way.

Her first year on the job, one of her coworkers had stabbed her in the back, telling everyone at the office she was shaking her ass up the corporate ladder. That little rumor had forced her to work twice as hard as everyone else. And even then, it had taken months for people to stop whispering behind her back.

"I'm serious, Liv. There's more to life than work, you know.

And you can bet your ass the job won't keep you warm at night, so I'm going to let you in on one of life's little secrets, okay? When you die, no one's going to care if it says partner, or president, or fry cook on your epitaph."

Chloe shifted on her stool and tossed a handful of dark curls over her shoulder. She scanned the bar subtly.

Always trolling for a man, Olivia thought as she watched her friend.

Chloe had the curves of a bygone era and had yet to find a man who could handle them. Then again, maybe it wasn't her curves that were the problem. Chloe had a larger-than-life personality and when her heart-shaped lips parted, there was no telling what might come pouring out.

"When Pritchard promotes you on Monday—"

"Don't you mean *if* Pritchard promotes me?" Olivia corrected. "There's no guarantee."

"Whatever." As usual, Chloe was quick to waive off the voice of reason. "Pritchard practically promised you that partnership if you landed the Bianchi account, which you did. Besides, what else could he want to see you about?"

"Who knows?"

Olivia rolled her shoulders, trying to ease the tension that had settled in and taken up permanent residence. Under normal circumstances, she thrived under pressure.

Too bad these weren't normal circumstances.

Ever since Pritchard sent her the cryptic meeting request, she'd been wound tighter than a Manhattan face lift. She *deserved* this promotion. She wanted this partnership so bad she could taste it.

It tasted a hell of a lot like humble pie, which she'd be too happy to serve up to her family on a silver Tiffany platter.

Chloe made a rude noise in the back of her throat and scrunched up her nose. "God knows it's not like the old toad to skip his Monday morning squash game. He's definitely up to something."

Olivia shot her friend a disapproving look.

Pritchard wasn't *that* bad.

Sure, he was a little temperamental, but he had a good heart and had always treated her fairly. He'd given her a shot five years ago and she'd stand by him as long as he did the same for her. Even so, with the meeting weighing on her mind, Olivia didn't know how she was going to get through the weekend.

"Can we please talk about something else? I don't want to get my hopes up for nothing."

For good reason.

Thrust into beauty pageants from the time she could walk, Olivia had been crowned a Dairy Princess, an Apple Blossom Princess, and a hundred other ridiculous things she didn't care to remember. But it made her parents happy and earned money for college. Win-win, right?

Problem was, the more pageants she won, the less people actually saw *her*.

Olivia became known as a pageant princess, nothing more, nothing less.

It didn't matter she'd had the highest GPA in her class or that she was the editor of the high school newspaper. No one cared that she'd started the civic club or volunteered at the food bank. It didn't even matter that she'd been accepted to Cornell.

Any hope of being seen as more than a pretty face evaporated.

Back home, everyone assumed she'd become some rich businessman's trophy wife and live in a stupid house in the Hamptons.

Well, *screw* that.

She was writing her own plan and she'd done pretty damn

well for herself so far. She was successful, self-reliant, and happy. Mostly.

All she needed was this promotion.

And for people not to assume she'd slept her way to the top.

"Well, he'd be stupid not to promote you," Chloe continued, unfazed. "You've been busting your ass for the last five years." She paused as the waitress dropped off their drinks; a dry martini for Olivia and a Cosmopolitan for Chloe. "You deserve that promotion," she said, a wicked grin spreading across her face, "and a night of hot, dirty sex."

Choking on her drink, Olivia fixed her friend with a death glare she hoped would end the depressing conversation about her sex life, or notable lack thereof. She certainly didn't need a reminder that the only orgasms she'd had this year had come from a rose toy.

"Seriously, Liv. You deserve, like, a whole weekend of raunchy sex," Chloe assured her, head bobbing up and down. "The dirtier the better."

"Charming." Olivia rolled her eyes and opened the top button on her blouse.

Spring was in the air and the glass windows at the front of the bar had been rolled up, admitting a light breeze which kissed her skin as it floated across the open-air restaurant. It was her favorite time of year and she relished walking through the city's parks as they came to life at the end of a cold, slush-filled winter.

Of course, she could enjoy the changing season a lot more if Chloe would get off her back.

Guilt seized her at the thought.

Chloe meant well and she was a good friend to put up with Olivia's ridiculous work schedule.

Hell, without Chloe, she'd probably never leave the office.

Their friendship was basically the only thing that could

challenge her reputation as the office "Ice Queen"—not interested in making friends, definitely not interested in dating.

"Answer me this." Chloe's brown eyes sparkled with mischief and Olivia worked to suppress a groan. No need to guess where this line of questioning was headed. As if she'd read Olivia's mind, Chloe asked playfully, "When was the last time you got laid or even went on a date, Ice Queen?"

"Umm," she stalled. She knew the answer to the first question, but no way was she admitting that. As for the last date she'd been on? She really couldn't remember. Maybe Chad? He'd taken her to see the latest Hollywood thriller, which had totally sucked. It was their first and only date. "Last date? I went to the movies with Chad, that guy from the gym, last summer."

"Liv, that was two summers ago," Chloe returned quietly, a look of pity clouding her face.

"Oh, hell." Leaning back on her stool, she crossed her arms over her chest.

Had it really been that long? Did it even matter?

She was so close to reaching her goal. Dating could wait. She was only twenty-eight, after all, and she wasn't looking to get tied down any time soon.

Not that it looked like she was in any danger of that anyway.

"You know what I think?" Chloe asked, not bothering to wait for a reply. "You need to adjust your expectations."

"And you're going to help me with that?"

"Take it from me," Chloe grumbled. "I've got a long list of one-night stands to prove that a night of great sex doesn't equal 'I do'. Why deny your carnal urges? Look around," she gestured. "Are you really that oblivious to all this sexy man candy?"

"I appreciate a good-looking guy as much as the next girl, but—"

"Bullshit," Chloe argued, crossing her arms and giving her

ample breasts an unnecessary lift that was sure to turn a few heads.

"What? I do!"

"Oh, really?" Chloe smirked, locking eyes with Olivia. "Prove it, Ice Queen."

"Would you cut that out? What are you even talking about?"

"I dare you to seduce one of these delicious stud muffins," Chloe challenged, a lascivious grin transforming her face, "and I get to choose which one."

"Man candy? Stud muffins?" Olivia arched her brow. "Are you hungry? Do you need me to get you a snack?"

"I. Dare. You."

"You cannot be serious." Olivia scoffed, tapping her fingers idly on the table and avoiding Chloe's intense stare. "What are we, twelve? I am not going to have sex with some random guy on a dare."

"Your loss," Chloe chided, smiling coyly. "Don't you at least want to see what you're missing?"

Unable to deny her curiosity, she twisted in her chair hoping to catch a glimpse of the man who'd inspired such a ballsy challenge. When her gaze settled on Chloe's choice, she was sorry she'd looked.

The guy was insanely hot. Tall, broad shouldered, and oozing confidence, he was exactly the kind of guy she would be attracted to—*if* she were in the market for a one-night stand, which she wasn't.

Still, it was impossible to ignore the slow burn moving south from her belly as she drank in his smoldering good looks.

Shit. His gaze swung toward her and she knew she'd been caught staring. Real smooth.

She bit down on the inside of her cheek, refusing to shrivel under the heat of his gaze. She wasn't one of those girls. And judging by the light in his eyes, he kind of liked that. She couldn't quite make out the color, but their ravenous look left no doubt as to his intentions.

Olivia had never been a believer in lust at first sight, but apparently her body hadn't gotten the message.

Like a lit fuse, desire raced through her, awakening urges that had been dormant too long. Maybe Chloe was doing her a favor after all. It *had* been a while, and the prospect of having those masculine hands wrapped around her body instead of the stem of a martini glass *was* promising.

2

___

COLE

Cole Bennett eyed his martini with a mixture of appreciation and discontent, trying to decide if he should order another. The martini was damn near perfect, but it wasn't exactly his drink of choice. He preferred a nice smooth scotch every day of the week, but what the hell.

The night was young and he didn't have anywhere else to be.

It didn't hurt that he was getting top notch service from the busty, bottle-blond bartender he'd pegged for the actress/model type. He'd smile and tip her well, but that was as far as it would go. It was his first night back in New York, and he was determined to be on his best behavior.

More than anything, he was glad to be home.

Home meant a New York slice and more time with his sister, Anna. Growing up, he'd always looked out for her, but thirty-five hundred miles had forced him to step back and recognize her independence. Although he grudgingly accepted her adulthood, it was comforting to know he was only a short drive away if she needed him.

Sure, there were certain things he'd miss about London, but

his lifestyle was far better suited to the hustle and bustle of the Big Apple.

It was no secret to anyone who knew him that he lived on the edge, with his penchant for fast cars, hard liquor, and high stakes. After all, life was meant to be lived and he was determined to go full-throttle after what he wanted. It was that tenacity which had earned him his first million *and* nearly ruined him in London, where going after what—or rather, *who* —he'd wanted had nearly cost him everything he'd worked so hard to build.

That was a mistake he wouldn't be repeating, but it didn't mean he was going to settle down any time soon.

He nearly laughed at the thought.

For years, Anna had been bugging him to settle down and start a brat pack of his own, but there was no way in hell that was happening.

Cole Bennett didn't settle for anything.

Besides, hadn't fantasizing about that happily-ever-after bullshit been what had burned him in London? He'd seen enough broken families, including his own, to know a fairytale when he saw one.

No, Cole liked his life just fine.

He especially liked the hot blonde he'd been admiring for the last half hour.

Too bad it was her sultry looking friend who was undressing him with her eyes.

He wasn't interested.

Cole set down his drink and focused on the blonde. She exuded class with a snug skirt that hugged her subtle curves and a hint of cleavage peeking through the open collar of her crisp white blouse. Just the thought of twisting his fingers in that honey blond ponytail had his palms itching.

And those legs. He had always been a leg man and hers were first-class all the way.

Fortunately for his newfound resolve, she didn't look like the one-night stand type.

She was completely focused on her friend and hadn't looked his way once.

Nor had she looked at anyone else in the crowded bar.

There was a time when he would have jumped at the challenge, but he was older and wiser now and had seen first-hand what kind of trouble that could bring. There were plenty of women who were looking for a night of great sex, no more and no less, so why borrow trouble by screwing with the ones who wanted more?

Shit. Who was he kidding?

If he sat here much longer, he'd have a full-blown hard-on at the mere thought of slipping between those thighs.

He needed to get that second drink or a change of scenery.

Without warning, her stool swiveled and she met him straight on, as though she'd felt the heat of his gaze all along. There was no mistaking the burning desire that flared in her clear blue eyes while she stared at him unabashedly.

Maybe he'd been wrong about her after all.

She was definitely interested, but would she act on the impulse?

3

OLIVIA

Hoping to calm her unsteady nerves, Olivia sucked in a deep breath as she approached the bar.

Was she really doing this? And oh, god, what if she made a complete fool of herself? What if he wasn't interested? Maybe she'd imagined the spark between them?

She exhaled slowly.

Confidence in the bedroom had never been an issue for her, but she'd also never set out to seduce a complete stranger before. She was out of her league and it took all her self-restraint not to glance back at the table where Chloe was waiting for the check.

What was the big deal anyway?

It wasn't like she'd be giving up her virginity, for crying out loud. Her v-card was long gone, no thanks to the ineptitude of Danny Reid and one highly overrated prom.

This was just sex.

As long as she remembered how to do it, things would be fine.

Probably.

When she stepped up to the heavily lacquered bar, the perky

blond bartender was quick to take her order.

"What'll you have, hun?" she asked as she wiped down the scarred counter.

"Dirty martini," Olivia replied without hesitation.

If she was going down the path of seductress, she might as well put on her big girl panties and commit one hundred percent.

She hated to admit it, but there was no escaping a childhood spent chasing pageant crowns without learning a thing or two about catching someone's eye.

Olivia zeroed in on the TV above the bar as she waited for her drink.

The Penguins and Rangers were duking it out in a particularly brutal looking 3rd period. She didn't have much time for sports and knew just enough about hockey to be dangerous in conversation, but it helped settle her frayed nerves nonetheless.

Nothing like a bunch of hulking, over-sexed guys slugging it out to set a girl at ease.

"How much?" she asked when the bartender returned with her liquid courage.

"No charge," the blonde replied through suddenly tight lips. "The gentleman at the end of the bar took care of it."

"Oh, well, thanks." Olivia felt a slow flush creep into her cheeks as she turned and smiled at the sexy stranger.

He dipped his head in acknowledgement and a wave of dark hair fell over his forehead.

Her pulse thundered.

And here she'd thought he couldn't get any hotter. So much for that.

At least she had an opening now. After all, he'd just bought her a drink. It would be rude not to thank him personally, wouldn't it?

Olivia made her way to the end of the bar.

She chose the stool to his left and sat down without asking permission. He was alone and looking for company. The martini she held in her right hand was proof of that.

"Are you always in the habit of buying drinks for strangers?" she asked, crossing her legs and bumping his in the process.

Their knees brushed and electricity flowed through her like a current, reminding her just how long it had been since a man had touched her.

"Just the pretty ones," he returned with a cocky grin.

Worst. Line. *Ever*.

Olivia burst out laughing, releasing the nervous energy that had collected in the pit of her stomach.

He might be to-die-for gorgeous, but his pickup game could use some work.

"If that's the best you've got, it's no wonder you're sitting here alone on a Friday night," she teased, relaxing in spite of herself.

"You're smiling, aren't you?" he asked, raking a hand through his inky black hair and pushing the loose strand back from his forehead.

"Yeah, well, I don't get out much," she replied, holding his gaze.

Up close, she was surprised to discover his eyes were a startling shade of gunmetal gray. They were like nothing she'd ever seen before. The color was a sharp contrast to his fair skin and dark hair, but it had nothing on his smile. She'd always been a sucker for good teeth and dimples, and he had both behind that five o'clock shadow.

The devilish grin he flashed hooked up on the right side and her pulse soared.

She prayed he couldn't feel the heat rolling off her.

If a bump of the knee and a flash of dimples made her feel this way, what would it be like to *really* touch him?

She wanted to find out. Whether or not she could handle it was an entirely different question.

"One of those all work and no play types?" His words hung between them, heavy with sexual suggestion.

Any other day she would have dismissed the line, but not tonight. His boldness had her stomach churning and her heart racing. This was a man used to getting what he wanted and tonight he wanted *her*.

It was a heady feeling unlike any other.

"Something like that," she replied.

"Then it must be my lucky day. Cole Bennett," he offered, reaching to shake her hand. "And you are?"

"Olivia Masterson." She met him halfway, her delicate hand slipping inside of his as he enveloped her fingers in warmth.

A tingle danced over her skin and she felt her cheeks redden at his touch.

There was no doubt about it—Cole Bennett was the sexiest man she'd ever laid eyes on.

"Very nice to meet you, Olivia Masterson." He released her hand, leaving a pang of disappointment. She wanted that tingle back, damn it! "You see, it's my first night in the city, so it must be luck our paths crossed, seeing as how you don't get out much."

"Oh, really?"

"True story," he swore, placing his hand over his heart and drawing her eyes south to his muscular shoulders and broad chest. He wore an expensive Italian suit that reeked of money, but it did little to hide his solid torso. If anything, the tailored jacket emphasized his perfection. "I just moved from England," he explained.

"And yet you have no accent." She plucked an olive from her glass. "Too bad. Women love a man with a sexy accent. Find them irresistible, actually. I'd say a British accent would do wonders for your otherwise lacking pickup lines."

Unable to resist goading him, she slipped the olive between her glossy lips and smiled, curious to see how he'd respond.

"Sexy *and* sassy. A dangerous combination in my experience," he mused as he studied her.

She gave him her best 'who me?' look and sipped her martini.

"Can I tell you a secret, Olivia?" His tone was conspiratorial as he leaned in, turning his smoky eyes on her.

She didn't know much about the fine art of seduction, but she knew shrinking wallflowers weren't sexy. Refusing to back down and determined to make good on the dare, she closed the gap between them, leaning forward until their shoulders brushed. She raised her brow in reply.

"I thought your friend was never going to leave."

"Is that right?" she asked, smiling as she drew out her inner flirt. "Better watch your manners, Cole Bennett, or a girl might get the sense you don't play well with others."

"I don't," he growled. His gaze rolled over Olivia, lingering on her mouth. There was no doubt about his meaning, or the tension simmering between them. She fought the urge to lick her lips, wondering if he tasted as sinfully good as he looked. "When I see something I want, I find a way to make it mine. And I'll be damned if I'm going to share."

His expression was hunger in its purest and basest form.

She swallowed, not trusting her voice as a torrent of desire surged from between her legs. She couldn't remember the last time a man had made her feel so sexy.

Forget the dare. She was riding a wave of pure, animalistic need that demanded to be unleashed.

It didn't make any sense.

She was as straitlaced as they came, and Cole was a virtual stranger, but Olivia wanted him more than she'd wanted any man in a very long time. It didn't matter that she didn't know what he did or where he lived. It only mattered that she know what he felt like inside her.

She took a final sip from her martini glass, solidifying her resolve.

Her heart hammered so hard in her chest she was sure he would know she was a fraud. She was probably the only twenty-eight-year-old in the city who couldn't check the 'one-night stand' box on her resume.

That was about to change.

"Your place or mine?"

Surprise flickered across his face, but was quickly replaced by a grin.

Her heart fluttered and she was grateful for the support of the stool. Without it she would've surely melted into a hapless puddle on the floor of the bar.

Cole Bennett had a killer smile.

"I've got a room at the hotel across the street."

"Perfect," she replied, slipping off the stool and planting her feet firmly on the hardwood floor.

He pulled out his wallet and threw a hundred dollar bill on the bar.

In one swift motion, he placed his hand on the small of her back and turned her toward the door. Before she could think too much about what she was doing, he was gently guiding her through the bar and out onto the busy sidewalks of Manhattan with a gesture that spoke of possession.

They didn't talk much as they made their way across the street and through the hotel lobby.

It was a comfortable silence, but the anticipation building within her was unbearable.

She was enjoying the warmth of Cole's touch on her back, but she wanted more—*much more.*

4

COLE

Cole watched the elevator creep down to the lobby and silently cursed his room on the 35th floor.

Why hadn't he booked a room on a lower level? The answer was obvious, but as he admired Olivia's reflection in the gold-plated doors ahead, he cursed again.

Truthfully, he hadn't thought she'd have the guts to leave with him, but now that they were in the hotel, he was going to make damn sure she had an unforgettable night. Olivia was sexy as hell and he wasn't taking any chances. He had to know if she felt half as good on the inside as she looked on the outside.

When the elevator finally reached the landing, the doors opened with a quiet *whoosh* and he stepped inside.

He turned to see her hesitate briefly and his stomach dropped.

Indecision was written all over her face, but damn, she was beautiful even with doubt clouding those baby blues. He wanted to take her in his arms and show her what she'd be missing, but this had to be her choice.

His erection strained against the unyielding fabric of his dress pants.

Christ, if she walked away now, he'd be taking one hell of a cold shower.

His patience was rewarded when she stepped forward, a half-smile lighting her slender face. He reached for her hand and pulled her close as her fingers interlaced with his.

"Which floor?" she asked, reaching for the control panel with her other hand.

"Thirty-five." He paused as she pressed the button. "You know, I was starting to think you'd changed your mind," he murmured, sliding his free arm around her waist and pressing her body to his.

Olivia was tall, maybe 5'9", but with heels, she was just the right height to rest her head on his shoulder.

"Are you calling me a tease?" she challenged, tipping her head back to look him in the eye.

Her breasts swelled against his chest with the change of position, and his cock strained even harder against the zipper of the unforgiving pants.

"Wouldn't dream of it." He brought his hand to her mouth, dragging his thumb roughly across her full bottom lip. He felt a shiver race down her spine as her hips arched toward him. "But I'd be lying if I said I wasn't thinking about all the ways I'm going to make you come."

Before she could reply, he pressed her against the side of the elevator and brought his mouth to her ear. "And I always get what I want, Olivia Masterson."

When his hand slid up her back, his mouth descended on the soft flesh of her neck.

He placed a soft kiss just below her ear and traced a line down the gentle curve of her neck with his tongue, savoring the sweetness of her skin. She tasted like a summer breeze, light and sweet. How it was possible, he didn't know and didn't care. He just wanted more.

He nipped at her skin, pinching it gently between his teeth, and she sighed with pleasure, her body melting into his.

There was a lot of repressed sexuality under her businesslike exterior and he suspected it had been a while since she'd allowed herself to give in to passion and lose herself in a man's embrace. He moved his mouth up Olivia's neck and chin, coming to rest on her lips. She responded savagely, her tongue darting into his mouth with surprising intensity.

Oh, yeah, she would definitely be a screamer.

A bell chimed, shattering his concentration.

He'd nearly forgotten they were in the elevator, and was on the verge of tearing her clothes off. Desperate to get behind closed doors where he could do all sorts of wicked things to her, he pulled back from her grip.

Undeterred by the lack of privacy, she grabbed his silk tie and led the way with the confidence of a woman who was about to get *exactly* what she wanted.

5

OLIVIA

THE DOOR FELL SHUT behind Olivia and she knew the time for second thoughts had passed. Not that she was having second thoughts, exactly. More like nerves. Like a bad case of I-haven't-had-sex-in-three-years-and-I-hope-I-remember-how-to-do-it-right nerves.

Cole, on the other hand, looked perfectly at ease as he moved purposefully through the penthouse suite.

She followed him, unnerved at the opulence. Travertine floors. Marble topped bar. And was that? No, it couldn't be. A baby-*freaking*-grand piano.

The place made her apartment in Midtown look like a flop house by comparison.

He tossed his jacket on the back of a chair and loosened his tie.

When he turned his attention to her, all rational thought evaporated under the heat of his stare. As he crossed the room, her heart fluttered and her breath hitched uneasily. The slow burn that had been circulating through her all evening simmered just below the surface, crackling like fire as a rush of adrenaline was released.

"There's nothing sexier in the world than a woman who knows what she wants and isn't afraid to ask for it," he murmured, cupping her chin and raising her lips to his. He stopped just short of kissing her. "Do you know what you want, Olivia?"

"Yes," she breathed, wondering if he wasn't the real tease. She hadn't come here to talk, and judging by the bulge in his pants, neither had he.

"What do you want?" he asked as his hand skimmed the length of her neck and burned a trail down the front of her blouse.

The first button came undone with a flick of his fingers.

Olivia searched for a clever reply that wouldn't come.

His fingers moved deftly from one button to the next and she trembled with the longing to feel his mouth on her again, to taste his vodka-tinged lips.

"I should think it's obvious what I want," she gasped.

God, how could he think about words at a time like this?

All she could think about was the ache between her legs.

"I want to hear you say it," he commanded, moving his hands inside her blouse and over her breasts, gently massaging her nipples through the soft lace of her bra until they were fully hardened and begging for his kiss.

Cole kept his eyes locked on her as he worked her breasts, making it impossible to think about anything but her desperate need for him and the fact she despised the wretched clothes separating their bodies.

Olivia shrugged out of her blouse and his agile fingers unhooked the bra, baring her breasts for further exploration. He rolled her left nipple between his thumb and forefinger and she moaned with pleasure.

His hands were perfect—soft and gentle, but sure and firm at the same time.

It wasn't enough. She needed more and she needed it *now*.

Unable to wait any longer for the feel of his tongue, she guided him to the rosy bud.

She threw her head back and whimpered as he sucked her into his warm mouth, circling her breast with his tongue. Only when he closed his teeth over the peak in a playful bite did she look down to meet his eyes.

"I want to hear you say it," he repeated, his words swirling seductively through her head, creating images so dirty she didn't dare speak them aloud. "Tell me what you want me to do to you, or we're done here."

Oh, god. She had never been the type to talk dirty or even really articulate her needs, but she was fairly certain, judging by the determined look in his eye, that he might call the whole damn thing off if he didn't get his way right here, right now.

Only that wasn't an option.

"Tell me, Olivia."

She licked her lips and brought his face back up to hers. Kissing him with a ferocity that had been suppressed too long, her mouth slanted over his without restraint. She grabbed the back of his head and ran her fingers through his unruly hair, enjoying its softness, as her tongue parted his lips. When he tried to pull back, she held on tighter, biting down firmly on his lower lip in retaliation.

"I want to feel you inside me. I want you to give me a mind-blowing orgasm the likes of which I've never experienced before and I don't care how you do it. Are we sufficiently clear now?"

A low growl rolled off his lips. "Do you want my fingers?" he asked, unzipping her skirt and letting it drop to the carpeted floor.

"Yes," she whispered, thankful she had chosen to wear a thong with the fitted skirt and not granny panties.

Cole ran his hands over her bare backside, which he palmed and used to pull her close.

His erection pressed firmly against her belly and she forgot all about her panties.

"What about my tongue?" He sank to his knees, running his mouth down her stomach from her navel.

Her bare flesh prickled when his tongue made its way south. "Yes."

She was vaguely aware that she was down to panties and heels and hadn't gotten even one of his buttons undone. It was hard to care when he was touching her like this, though.

"What about my cock?" he teased, looking up at her as his skilled fingers tugged at the waistband of her lacy underwear. Taking extra care to caress every inch of her feverish skin along the way, he pulled them down.

Her body shook with anticipation.

"*Yes*," she begged, desperate to ease the ache he'd created, and willing to take whatever pleasure he was offering.

When his hands slid back up her calves, he forced her knees apart, leaving her fully exposed.

She sighed as he pulled her hips to his face and kissed her, nearly sending her to orgasm at the first touch. She had never been so ready for a man in her life. She needed Cole Bennett inside her *right-freaking-now*.

He started off slow, teasing her with the promise of ecstasy, until her body responded to their undeniable chemistry. When her hips rocked involuntarily and invited him deeper, he became ravenous. He *devoured* her. There was no other way to describe the heavenly sensation as he licked and probed, swirling around her clit and sucking her to the brink of madness.

He seemed to know her body in a way first-time lovers could never know one another, applying the perfect amount of pressure in all the right places. And the things he was doing with his tongue, dear god, where had he learned that?

Her body quivered as the tension built within her, threatening to explode in orgasm. She laced her fingers through his hair, bringing him to a halt.

He looked up at her from below heavily lidded eyes ripe with desire.

"Not without you," she panted. "I want to feel you come inside me. I need you inside me."

Cole was on his feet in an instant.

Olivia went straight for the belt as he tore through the buttons on his shirt. She had the buckle undone in record time and barely stopped to register his sculpted abs. Desperate to free his erection and feel every last inch of him within her, she fought her way past the zipper. Before shedding the last of his clothing, he pulled a condom from his wallet.

He ripped it open and rolled it over his length.

Holy crap! The man was *huge*.

Olivia gave silent thanks for foreplay and lubricated condoms even though she was more than ready for him.

Anxious to resume her ascent to orgasm, she reached for him, but he pushed her up against the wall, her back flattened against the textured silk fabric that lined the room. He gently brushed his knuckles across her cheek, down her neck, and across her shoulders, eventually tangling them in the mass of hair that hung down her back.

"You are so fucking beautiful."

The emotion smoldering in his eyes was unnerving. How could a man she barely knew make her feel this way?

Free, uninhibited, cherished.

Unsure of what to say and not wanting to ruin the moment, she wrapped her left leg around his waist. Tilting her hips, she opened herself to him, offering the only thing she had to give.

She knew little more than his name, but it was enough. She felt more comfortable and alive with Cole than she'd felt with any of her past boyfriends.

"Sweetheart, I'm going to fuck you like you've never been fucked before." He didn't waste any time delivering on that promise.

He pressed forward, driving deep into her with the first stroke.

Blistering heat tore through her.

She sucked in a sharp breath, her body adjusting to his size.

No man had ever filled her so completely and the feeling was exquisite. His hand slipped from her hair and came to rest on the underside of her rear, supporting her weight. She wrapped her other leg around him, locking her ankles and taking his full length.

His hips slammed into hers over and over with deliciously perfect rhythm.

Olivia fought to keep her orgasm at bay with every thrust deep within her. She didn't want to come too soon, but it was impossible to fight the rising pressure as their bodies rocked in unison. As their flesh came together, she was surprised to discover a feeling she hadn't expected to find in Cole's smoky eyes: *intimacy*.

"Cole," she said, trying to warn him but failing as her body exploded in sensation.

Powerful waves of ecstasy rolled through her and brought her to the edge of bliss and back again.

She gave into the pleasure, screaming his name and digging her nails into his shoulder.

"That's right, I want to feel you come all around me." He gave a feral growl and a final thrust before succumbing to his own orgasm.

Cole's body shuddered and his grip on Olivia tightened. He

held her pinned against the wall, their sweaty bodies pressed seamlessly together a moment longer while he caught his breath.

He brushed a strand of damp hair from her forehead and smiled. "I knew you'd be a screamer."

Refusing to be ashamed of her enthusiastic orgasm, Olivia laughed.

She was a modern woman, after all. She could handle a night of great sex with no strings.

Then Cole did something completely unexpected—he placed a tender kiss on her forehead. For a moment she felt connected to him on a level much deeper than the physical bond they'd shared.

6

COLE

COLE SLIPPED QUIETLY from bed and pulled on his boxers. He was damn thirsty and didn't want to disturb Olivia, who was still sound asleep and breathing softly from deep under the down comforter. In the bathroom, he flipped on the light and flinched as the harsh glow of the overhead bulb assaulted his eyes.

Shit.

Given the nightly rate for a penthouse suite, surely the hotel could afford better lighting.

He gave himself a moment to adjust and grabbed one of the glasses from the sink. He filled it with tap water, having exhausted the supply of bottled water in the suite's fridge. Olivia's appetite for sex was matched only by her enthusiasm and he was bordering on dehydration.

The woman was insatiable.

They were three-for-three in the orgasm department and he was getting hard again just thinking about her lying naked in the next room.

It was turning out to be a hell of a first night back in the city.

Draining the glass, he stared at his reflection in the mirror. His hair was a mess, sticking up at odd angles, and he could use a shave, but that would come later. He needed a few more hours of sleep before he'd be ready to face the day. He refilled the glass and leaned into the vanity, thinking about Olivia.

He'd been with a lot of women, but not like this. Never like this.

He wasn't exactly sure why it was different, although there was usually more talking involved before a woman agreed to go home with him.

Not that he was complaining.

He knew he was good-looking, but in his experience, most women, even the ones who knew the score, liked to play hard-to-get. Maybe it was part of the thrill for them. Or maybe it was their way of dealing with society's double standard when it came to the rules of sex.

Either way, he wasn't judging.

He liked sex and he appreciated a woman who wasn't afraid to go after what she wanted, especially in the bedroom.

But what made Olivia different? Try as he might, he couldn't put his finger on it.

She emanated class, and he was certain this wasn't characteristic behavior for her. That much was evident in her nerves.

The fact she'd nearly bolted in the lobby said it all.

No, this definitely wasn't her typical Friday night.

His rebound radar kicked in then, but he dismissed it immediately. It didn't feel right.

She didn't have the desperate air of a woman nursing a broken heart, or of one looking to get even with a cheating boyfriend.

Well, whatever the hell was going on with her, he liked it. *A lot.*

Smiling, he flipped off the bathroom light. He would definitely have to get her number in the morning.

After all, he hadn't been in Manhattan for years. It wouldn't hurt to have a gorgeous woman to show him around.

As he slid back under the covers, she rubbed her bare ass up against him.

Christ. The woman was going to kill him, but he wasn't about to deny her.

7

———

OLIVIA

OLIVIA STRETCHED LAZILY and rolled to her side. Screw the gym. It was Saturday and she was sleeping in. It wouldn't kill her to miss one day on the treadmill.

She deserved a break.

Maybe she'd even go for brunch.

She was starving and the thought of Belgian waffles with fresh blueberries and crème had her stomach rumbling.

The more she thought about it, the more she was convinced she deserved to treat herself.

She could take her e-reader and sit on the patio of that cute little café down the block. She'd always wanted to eat there, but had never made the time.

Of course, that plan would require getting out of bed.

As she peeked out from beneath sleep laden lashes, debating the merits of sleep vs. food, reality came crashing back.

Olive or Twist. The dare. *Cole.*

Holy. Shit. She'd really done it.

Chloe would never believe her. If it weren't for the super-hot, super-naked man lying next to her, she wouldn't believe it herself. Knowing Chloe, she'd want photographic evidence, but she sure as hell wasn't going there just to convince her friend.

Olivia lay still, barely daring to breathe for fear of waking him.

She studied his profile and smiled to herself. He had a wicked case of bed head, but it only seemed to add to his sexiness, something she was sure he wouldn't say about her if he woke up and saw the tangled mess that was her own hair.

After a quick look at his muscular chest, she resisted the urge to run her tongue over his pecs, down his hard stomach, and up over his... *No! Bad idea*, she scolded her inner sex kitten.

He'd wake up and then, well, she knew what would happen: morning sex.

And while she wasn't fundamentally opposed to morning sex, her vagina might feel differently after the marathon session last night.

How did a guy who practically screamed Wall Street get a body like that anyway?

She sighed at the injustice of it all.

Sex with Cole had been un-*freaking*-believable.

She had never had two orgasms, let alone four, in one night before. There was no doubt about it, he was hands-down the best lover she'd ever had, and despite the lack of actual sleep, she felt pretty damn good.

Still, she was in the penthouse suite of a complete stranger, a guy she'd had crazy monkey sex with and whom she sort of hoped wouldn't engage in any awkward morning-after talk.

Maybe she could sneak out while he was still sleeping.

It was a cowardly thing to do, but what the hell. There would be plenty of time to overanalyze the whole thing later. She'd be much more comfortable questioning her sanity and decision-making skills from the privacy of her own bed.

Peeling back the comforter, Olivia dropped her feet to the plush carpet and slipped from bed as carefully as she could to avoid waking him. He was sprawled on his back and, thankfully, dead to the world. She tiptoed to the living room to collect her clothes.

It didn't take long to figure out she was short one bra.

"Damn!" She scanned the dark room again.

Where could it be?

She'd looked everywhere.

Well, everywhere except the bedroom, although she doubted it had made it that far.

It was her favorite bra, but it was a sixty-five-dollar piece of luxury she was willing to sacrifice in order to avoid waking him. They'd had an amazing night together, but that didn't mean she wanted to hang around and chat about it.

Hell, she could hardly wrap her mind around the fact she'd actually done it.

No, what she needed right now was to put her brain on lockdown and focus on getting out of there before he woke up.

After grabbing her purse, she shut herself in the bathroom. She put on her wrinkled clothes, quickly tugged a brush through her hair and refastened her ponytail.

Time to steel herself for a swift, ninja-like exit.

She cracked the bathroom door and peeked out, relieved to find he was still sound asleep.

They hadn't slept much and there was a good chance he'd sleep late into the morning, but she wasn't planning to stick around to find out. Opening the door just enough to slip through, she forced herself to walk slowly from the room, despite the urge to make a mad dash for it. The last thing she needed was for him to wake up and find her running out the door like a lunatic.

When she reached the front door to the suite, she did a

mental happy dance and threw the lock back as gingerly as possible.

The bolt slid back with a loud *thwack*, ringing through the suite like a gunshot.

She held her breath, praying he hadn't heard.

After counting to three, she opened the door carefully, closed it, and hung the *Do Not Disturb* sign on the outside knob.

Safely in the hall, she sighed with contentment while she waited for the elevator.

In a few short minutes she'd return to the real world, losing herself in the city's masses, the warm glow of great sex plastered all over her face.

She hated to admit it, but if this was what the walk of shame felt like, she just might be able to get used to it.

Too bad she'd never see Cole again. They'd had an incredible night together and she'd felt connected to him.

Scratch that.

This was a one-shot deal—one night only, no repeat performances. She needed to get her head on straight and forget about Cole Bennett. This was going to be a big week, possibly the biggest of her life.

Now was the time to remain focused, not turn into some sex-crazed nympho.

By this time Monday, he would be a distant memory—one she seriously doubted any other man could live up to—but a memory nonetheless. That's just how it had to be.

8

COLE

CiOLE ROLLED over and reached for Olivia, wondering how she felt about morning sex.

Unfortunately, all he got for his efforts was a handful of the overstuffed down comforter, which definitely wasn't going to get the job done.

He sat up, quickly scanning the room.

The open bathroom door confirmed what he already knew: she'd bailed on him. No need to check the living room. Olivia was gone and chances were she wouldn't be returning with a piping hot cup of coffee.

Normally he'd be relieved at the prospect of not having to deal with awkward morning-after pleasantries, but he'd never had a chance to get her number.

Plus, he had another problem. He was hard as a rock.

There wasn't much he could do about the latter except take a cold shower and let nature run its course, but damn if he didn't feel disappointed—and a little insulted—at Olivia sneaking out.

Would it have killed her to say goodbye? He knew she'd had a good time last night. There was no denying her responsiveness or the pleasure they'd given one another.

So what then? Was she having second thoughts about her decision to come back to his room?

Wouldn't that be a kick in the balls.

He'd just about decided last night he wanted to take her to dinner. The urge to unravel the mystery that was Olivia Masterson was pretty damn strong. Even stronger was the urge to explore their scorching chemistry in the bedroom.

He had her first and last name. It would be easy enough to track her down...except that was creepy and probably qualified as stalking. And Cole Bennett definitely wasn't *that* guy. He didn't have to chase women; they'd always come to him freely, no strings attached.

"Shit," he groaned, falling back on the bed and slinging an arm across his face.

He needed to get a grip.

One night in the city and he was pining like a teenage girl? No fucking way.

There were millions of women in New York and he wasn't about to get hung up on one woman, no matter how great her ass was.

It wasn't his style.

Sure, Olivia was exciting, but it was just sex.

From the time he'd lost his virginity at sixteen, he had never had a problem getting women to drop their panties—the ones who wore them, anyway. With one major exception, he'd always had casual flings. He was good at them. They were so much easier. And he'd created some guiding principles to keep him out of trouble.

Rule #1: No staying for breakfast. Ever. Breakfast was a game changer. It was like a daytime date that gave women the impression things were getting serious. Then they started getting ideas about the future and relationships, which inevitably screwed up the sex.

Rule #2: Don't plan anything more than three days in advance. The three-day rule kept things casual. He never saw the same woman more than once a week and never got roped into weddings or other volatile events that had the potential to blow up like an emotional minefield.

Rule #3: No commitments. If she wants to have 'the talk', it's time to get the hell out.

The rules were simple. They ensured things never got too serious and no one got hurt.

He glanced at the clock on the nightstand.

It was only ten, so he had plenty of time for a trip to the hotel gym before meeting his realtor. The hotel was convenient, but it wasn't a great long-term set up. He needed to find an apartment, and experience had taught him it could take some time with his discerning taste and busy work schedule.

That meant he needed to stop thinking about Olivia and start thinking about more practical things like finding a place to live. If only he could get the sound of her screaming his name out of his head.

9

———

OLIVIA

OLIVIA'S PHONE VIBRATED UNCONTROLLABLY, sliding across the kitchen counter and threatening to take a dive to the slate floor below if she didn't answer it, *right now*. She considered tossing it in the utensil drawer, but knew that wouldn't put an end to Chloe's endless calls.

There was only one way to do that, and it meant answering the phone.

"Hey." She did her best to sound casual, despite the fact she'd been dreading this call. Well, this call and the six before it.

Olivia knew she couldn't hide forever, but she'd given it her best shot. Problem was, Chloe tended to be relentless when she wanted something, and the odds were good she was going crazy trying to figure out if Olivia had actually gone through with the dare.

"She lives!" Chloe sounded put out by the need to make a seventh phone call. Hard to blame her. "I was seriously starting to wonder. I almost called the police, you know."

"You almost called the police?" She bit back a laugh. "Because the text message I sent didn't put your overactive imagination at ease?"

"I'm fine. Call you later." Chloe's words dripped with sarcasm. "Not so much. For all I knew the guy had you bound and gagged with one of those strappy little ball things!"

"A ball gag?" Olivia offered and burst out laughing. It was unlikely Chloe would have called the police. On the other hand, she did sound pretty ticked off that Olivia hadn't answered her phone all day. "I'm sorry I scared you," she apologized, feeling a twinge of guilt. "I had some errands to run, but I should have called sooner."

"Damn straight!" Chloe agreed, perking up. "Now, you can make it up to me by sharing all the juicy details from last night. And don't even think about leaving anything out."

"Wouldn't dream of it," she replied, rolling her eyes.

Walking to the fish bowl on the kitchen counter, she dropped some fish bits in Rufus's bowl. Her busy schedule didn't allow for a four-legged pet, but she didn't mind. Rufus, the colorful Betta fish who shared her apartment, was the perfect roommate. They had such clear relationship parameters. He didn't talk back, and he wasn't too needy.

And unlike Chloe, he didn't require intimate details of her sex life.

"Well?" Chloe prompted. "Quit stalling, Liv. Did you do the deed or what?"

"Yes," she admitted, her cheeks flaming with embarrassment at the omission. God, was she really blushing like a virgin? How ridiculous. She was twenty-eight years old, for crying out loud. She could have guilt-free sex with whomever she wanted, couldn't she?

"Eeee!" Chloe squealed, piercing her eardrums. "I knew it! I *knew* it!"

Olivia held the phone at arm's length, waiting for Chloe to get it out of her system.

She loved Chloe like a sister, but at times like this, she was thankful for her status as an only child. If twenty-five-year-old Chloe behaved this way, she could only imagine what a handful sixteen-year-old Chloe must've been.

"Done now?" she asked, cautiously bringing the phone back to her ear.

"Depends," Chloe said, sounding like a bipolar chipmunk, all traces of her sullen attitude completely erased. "Are you going to give me the scoop or not?"

"What do you want me to say? That we went back to his hotel and had dirty, kinky sex all night long?"

"Umm, yeah." Chloe sighed. "Man, he was hot. I bet it was amazing. Why can't I meet a guy like that?"

"You meet guys like Cole all the time. The one night—"

"Cole?" Chloe asked, cutting her off. "Even his name is sexy! Are you going to see him again? You have to see him again, Liv. He could be *the one!*"

"No, I really don't, and he is definitely not *the one.*"

Was Chloe seriously trying to marry her off to some random bar guy after one night? The sex had been good, but it hadn't been *that* good. Or maybe it had been. Either way, it didn't matter, since she'd never see him again.

"Please don't tell me you didn't get his number."

"Okay, I won't."

"Liv! Have I taught you nothing?" Chloe whined. "Seriously, I can't believe I'm hearing this."

"Sorry to disappoint you," she said, unable to believe her ineptitude at dating was Chloe's biggest problem. "What can I say? I suck at life."

Chloe grumbled something unintelligible under her breath. "You know, I was really hoping you were going to turn over a new leaf."

"The kind where I have indiscriminate sex with total strangers?" Olivia asked, laughing in spite of herself.

"Beggars can't be choosers," Chloe conceded. "Any sex would be a step in the right direction."

"I'll tell you what. We can revisit the topic of my love life when I get that partnership. Until then, dating just isn't a priority."

10

OLIVIA

Olivia nursed her coffee and sifted through emails. Her meeting with Pritchard was just minutes away, and she was too nervous to manage much else this morning. Taking a deep breath, she closed her eyes and imagined her name on the door beside Jonathan's.

Pritchard, Masterson, & Associates.

All of her hard work was about to pay off, proving once and for all she belonged in this world, and not upstate with her parents and their antiquated views on women. She was going to get partner, and *nobody* could say it had been for any other reason than that she was damn good at her job.

Her work load, which was already out of control, was likely to get even heavier. That meant no more wild nights or one-night stands. Even if Cole had given her the best orgasms of her life.

Problem was, she couldn't stop thinking about him, wondering if she'd made a mistake sneaking out.

Which was exactly why she needed to get back on track and put her focus one hundred percent on her work.

A message popped up on her screen, alerting her it was two minutes to ten.

Time to meet with Pritchard. It was now or never.

She rose from the desk and smoothed her black pencil skirt, hoping Pritchard wouldn't see through to her nerves. She doubted 'prone to panic attacks' was a quality he was seeking in his new partner, the individual he would groom to lead his company when he retired in a few years.

Olivia straightened her back and strode down the hall with confidence. She was relieved when Pritchard's admin Gabby waved her right in.

No waiting. That had to be a good sign.

She passed through the open door, pausing when she realized Pritchard already had someone in his office.

Odd, he hadn't mentioned anyone joining them. The hairs on the back of her neck began to bristle as Pritchard looked her way. His face lit up when he saw Olivia and she found herself smiling in return.

Jonathan could be a bit self-involved at times, but after five years of mentoring, she'd come to think of him as a father figure. Although, truth be told, he was nothing like her own father, who was just as likely to be found tinkering with his tractor as he was picking apples in the orchard.

No, Pritchard was nothing like that at all.

A city dweller at heart, Pritchard wore overpriced suits, had a trophy wife half his age, and maintained an overbooked social calendar. He kept his white hair clipped short, his fingernails manicured, and played squash every Monday.

Every Monday except this one.

"I apologize for the interruption," Olivia offered. "Gabby said to come right in. I didn't realize you were in a meeting."

"It's fine," Pritchard returned, motioning her forward from behind his heavy cherry desk. Behind him, an expansive wall of windows revealed storm clouds rolling into the city. Although she didn't care much for the clouds, she would have killed for those windows in her own office. With any luck, she'd have a new office with an equally breathtaking view by the end of the meeting. "Come on in. We were just talking about you."

"All good things I—"

She stopped dead in her tracks as the man sitting across from Pritchard turned in his chair, revealing his face. Silver eyes fell on her, registering the same overwhelming sense of shock that rocked her to the core. In that instant, the oxygen was sucked from the room.

Olivia couldn't breathe.

She couldn't think.

Couldn't move.

She blinked. Once. Twice. Three times.

The scene before her remained unchanged.

Broad shoulders. Unruly black hair. Killer dimples.

This could *not* be happening.

What the hell was Cole doing here? She wasn't supposed to see him again—*ever*. So what the hell was he doing in Pritchard's office?

"Have a seat." Pritchard once again waved her forward like a poodle in need of coaching. Seeing no other option, she complied silently, taking the overstuffed leather chair next to Cole. She managed to avoid looking him in the eye as she crossed her legs and sat stiffly by his side. "Olivia, I would like to introduce you to Cole Bennett, my new partner."

No, that couldn't be right. Did he just say partner?

She stared at Pritchard blankly. Speechless. Here he sat in his posh office, pleased as pie with his new partner, while he was ripping her dreams apart.

She felt as if her world had been tipped on its axis, throwing everything into chaos. Little black dots danced at the edges of her vision, making Pritchard, who was as sharp as they came, appear fuzzy. A fine sheen broke out on her forehead, the back of her neck, and that hollow spot right between her breasts.

Not good.

Olivia's stomach dropped. When it lurched back with the fury of a category five hurricane, she feared the contents of her breakfast might make an unwelcome appearance on Pritchard's desk.

"Cole, this is Olivia Masterson. Olivia's my right hand around the office and will be able to show you—"

"Excuse me."

Not giving a crap if Pritchard was offended by her hasty exit, she raced from the room and down the hall, throwing herself through the door of the ladies' restroom without an ounce of grace or dignity.

She quickly scanned the stalls, which, thankfully, were empty. Moving to the sink, she braced her hands against the porcelain bowl and took a deep breath. The face that stared back at her from the mirror was pale and ashen.

How could this be happening?

Not only was she not getting the partnership, but a man who knew her more intimately than most was? Talk about getting royally screwed. There was no way she could face Cole every day.

Or work under him, for that matter.

Olivia had worked so hard to keep her professional life and personal life separate. She'd spent the last five years rubbing elbows with the most eligible bachelors in the city and she'd never accepted one drink, dinner, show, or museum offer. Not even when the super-hot guy from finance had invited her to the invitation-only gallery opening of one of her favorite NY artists.

Compared to some of her peers, she'd been a freaking saint.

It wasn't fair. She broke the rules one freaking time and this is what happened?

Fate was a cruel-ass bitch.

Shaking with frustration and needing an outlet for her anger, she spun from the sink and kicked the metal trashcan with all the energy she could muster.

It banged against the wall, so she kicked it again for good measure.

The resounding clunk reverberated through the empty bathroom, bouncing off the tile floor and providing a much-needed reality check. As if her day wasn't crappy enough, she'd just scuffed the hell out of the Burberry heels she hadn't really been able to afford anyway. The trashcan hadn't fared so well either, and was now sporting a rather massive dent.

Stellar.

She'd be faced with the evidence of her meltdown every time she came to pee.

Olivia turned on the faucet and splashed cold water on her face.

She had to keep it together.

Okay, maybe it was a little late for that, but she could recover from this. She couldn't afford a total breakdown, seeing as how the floor wasn't going to swallow her up and put an end to the misery any time soon.

Sure, she'd been kicked in the teeth, but she wasn't a quitter. Hadn't she proven that time and again throughout the years, overcoming everything life had thrown at her? Cole Bennett would be no different. She would go back to Pritchard's office and hear what he had to say. Then she'd return to her desk and do her job.

Come hell or high water, she'd show Pritchard he'd made a mistake.

She could do this. She *had* to. What other choice did she have?

11

COLE

Fuck. Fuck. Fuck.

Cole hadn't believed his eyes, or his bad luck, when Olivia had walked into Pritchard's office. She was wearing a pair of black framed glasses and her hair was slicked back in a bun, but there was no mistaking those legs or the sway of her hips as she crossed the room. Damn, she had nice legs. He shouldn't have been looking, but he was only human. And just seeing those legs again got his blood pumping to areas best not roused in the office.

Eight million people in New York and she worked for Pritchard?

He'd have been less surprised if she'd showed up in nine months toting a baby on her hip.

No, this definitely wasn't how he pictured the morning playing out.

Judging by the look on Olivia's face as she'd stormed out of Pritchard's office, the feeling was mutual.

He had the distinct impression she'd rather be anywhere else. Not that he blamed her. He was pretty damn uncomfortable himself. But the more he thought about it, the more sense it made. After all, it was the receptionist downstairs who'd recommended Olive or Twist for happy hour.

It was practically in the lobby.

Odds were lots of people headed over there to unwind after a long week.

"I wonder what's gotten into her?" Pritchard mused aloud. "I hope she's okay. Olivia's the best of the lot, the consummate professional. She'll be an invaluable asset to you as you're getting acclimated. Smart as a whip and works twice as hard as anyone else on the team. I actually considered making her an equity partner before I heard you were looking to invest in New York."

Fuck.

Was Pritchard really that oblivious?

The least he could have done was let her down easily, in private. This couldn't possibly end well. He'd screwed her brains out *and* screwed her out of a promotion?

No wonder she looked like she was about to puke her guts out.

Guilt racked Cole. He never would have slept with her if he'd known. He could only imagine what she was thinking. Showing up to work and finding out your wild one-night stand was the new boss?

That would be a tough pill to swallow for anyone, but for a woman like Olivia?

It would be devastating.

He tuned Pritchard out as he tried to see a way out of the mess that had just become Pritchard, Bennett, & Associates. So much for learning his lesson across the pond—never mix business with pleasure.

Pritchard rattled on endlessly, but Cole didn't pay much attention until he stopped speaking abruptly. At first Cole thought he'd been asked a question, but then realized Pritchard's attention was directed elsewhere.

He twisted in his seat to discover Olivia had returned.

"Is everything okay?" Pritchard asked, rising from his chair. His words were rich with concern, momentarily overriding his usually gruff demeanor.

"Yes, I'm fine, Jonathan."

Olivia reclaimed the empty chair next to Cole, but didn't so much as cast a weary glance in his direction. She kept her eyes trained on Pritchard as she spoke, her voice taking on a hard edge. He noted some of her color had returned. She didn't have the flushed look he'd enjoyed Friday night, but at least she didn't look like death warmed over. It was a start.

"I'm so sorry about running out of here like that. I had something that didn't agree with me this weekend."

"Oh, not food poisoning, I hope?" Pritchard asked as he gracefully slid back into his chair.

"No, I don't think so," she returned in a dangerously sweet tone. "More like something rotten."

"If you need to take the day off—"

"That won't be necessary." She shook her head, dismissing the suggestion. "I just had to get it out of my system."

"Well, wherever you went, I hope you won't be going back."

"Mmm. It wasn't very memorable, so I can assure you it's a mistake I won't be repeating," she replied, turning cold eyes on Cole and acknowledging his presence for the first time.

Talk about going straight for the jugular.

Every fiber of his being bucked at the mocking of his sexual prowess, but he'd take his licks—*this time*. Olivia was hurt and angry and needed to lash out at someone. He could be that bastard.

It was a role he knew well.

The sick thing was, she'd just called him rotten and

lackluster, she was glaring daggers at him, but damn if he still didn't want her. An image of Olivia climaxing on the desk flashed through his head and he shut it down immediately. The last thing he needed to do was add a hard-on to the already awkward situation.

No, what he needed to do was steer clear of her, act like the other night had never happened and move on. That would be the smart thing to do.

On the other hand, he had never been all that smart when it came to women.

He wanted what he wanted, and damn the consequences.

He studied Olivia, admiring the long lines of her body and the determined set of her jaw. She was working hard to ignore him, and it was sexy as hell.

It only made him want her more.

They could still be good together—*if* he could get her to let her guard down.

Maybe this wouldn't be so bad after all. Chemistry like theirs was meant to be explored, not stamped out. Perhaps fate had intervened on his behalf. He *had* wanted to see her again. Not that she was likely to let him get within five feet of her—at least, not naked.

He'd have to work on that.

If everything Pritchard said was true, and it probably was since the old man was sparing with his praise, she was an incredibly valuable asset to the company. They couldn't afford to lose her. He would have to find a way to make things right between them.

If only to prove to himself that he hadn't completely fucked up again, pissing away his future like his old man.

Dissolving his partnership in London and relocating to New York hadn't exactly been the long-term plan, but then again, long-term plans didn't seem to work out for him. Pritchard had needed an influx of cash, and he'd needed a fresh start away from the memories London held.

PBA might have been a marriage of convenience, but he intended to make the most of it, bringing a portfolio of powerhouse clients and sinking the majority of his assets into the company. Despite recent cash flow problems, Jonathan had built a solid company with a great reputation in the advertising industry. Together, they would take PBA to the next level. He'd do whatever it took to make that happen, because the fact was, he had to succeed in New York.

And success meant fixing things with Olivia.

Maybe she just needed some time to adjust to his presence.

She was a passionate woman, but when the flames died down, who knew?

For Cole, there was only one certainty: the idea of having those legs wrapped around him again was tempting. Yes, he would definitely have to work on getting under Olivia's skin the way she'd gotten under his. But first he'd have to earn her trust, and that was going to be an uphill battle all the way.

12

OLIVIA

OLIVIA REMOVED her glasses and tossed them on the desk blotter. She closed her eyes and pinched the bridge of her nose. Her head was throbbing and the Tylenol stash she kept hidden in her top left drawer was depleted.

Thankfully, it was almost quitting time.

This would be a day for the record books, because she planned to be out the door by five-oh-one and on her way home to a nice bottle of merlot. She wasn't normally one to drown her sorrows in alcohol, but if Pritchard's earlier bombshell wasn't wine-worthy, what was?

A soak in the tub didn't sound half bad either.

She'd slough off the day and start fresh in the morning. Tomorrow would be a better day.

It certainly couldn't be any worse.

A knock at the door startled her. She didn't have any appointments scheduled, and no one dared come by her office this late for fear of getting sucked into an evening work session. Her team was strong, but none of them shared her dedication or drive. While Olivia lived to work, most of them favored Chloe's 'work to live' philosophy.

She opened her eyes to find Cole leaning on the doorjamb, arms crossed over his chest like he owned the place, which technically, he did now. The whole thing smacked of 'boys club'. He flashed her a dimpled smile that she suspected was meant to be disarming.

It only pissed her off more.

The man was insufferable. Did he really think a smile was all it would take to make up for... *everything?* Probably. It was obvious he relied on his good looks to get what he wanted, but she wouldn't be falling for that again.

"Yes?" she asked, the solitary word sounding cold and callous even to her own ears.

She definitely wouldn't be invited to join the welcoming committee any time soon. She'd never treated a coworker, let alone a superior, this way before, but she couldn't seem to reign in her attitude. He'd humiliated her and crushed her dreams. So what if he hadn't known what he was doing? The end result was still the same.

Couldn't he just stay out of her hair for one stinking day so she could lick her wounds and regroup in private?

"Can we talk?" he asked, stepping through the door and shutting it behind him in one fluid motion.

For a big guy, he moved with ease. She remembered just how graceful he could be when it suited him. Heat coursed through her body at the memory and she was thankful he couldn't read her mind. Just because her stupid body craved his touch, didn't mean she was going to give into the urge.

Her head would win out; it always did.

"It would appear I don't have much choice in the matter," she returned, ignoring her lusty impulses and focusing instead on her humiliation-fueled anger. "What can I do for you this evening, Mr. Bennett?"

"Mr. Bennett?" He snorted, and much to her disdain, even

that was kind of sexy. "I think we're beyond formalities, don't you?"

"I beg to differ. Pritchard won't be putting *my* name on the letterhead any time soon."

"I didn't come here to talk about stationery." He raked a hand through his hair and rubbed the back of his neck, looking uncertain for what was probably the first time in his perfect life. "Mind if I sit down?"

He crossed the small office in three long strides, not waiting for the invitation she would never extend. Smart man. He dropped into the chair across from her desk and crossed his legs, right ankle over left knee. She noted that in addition to sleek Italian suits, he favored overly polished Italian leather shoes.

Somehow he pulled it off without looking like a completely pretentious tool.

Loads of money and panty-dropping good looks?

No wonder he thought he was god's gift to the X chromosome.

Her gaze travelled from the pristine shoe and halfway up his muscular leg before she caught herself. She was heading toward no man's land, and nothing good would come from it.

"Suit yourself." Olivia sighed and leaned back in her chair. She needed to put some distance between them. Like it wasn't enough the man was walking sex, he even smelled irresistible. His scent, ginger and spice, was teasing her senses, reminding her of their night together, and chipping away at her resolve.

"I thought we should talk about the other night," he began cautiously. "You know, clear the air since we'll be working together?"

"There's nothing to talk about." Folding her hands, she placed them on the desk. She needed to be firm about this, make sure he got the message the first time. No way did she have it in her to have this conversation twice. "We're both adults."

"I wouldn't think it's quite that simple."

"Then you'd be wrong." He was trying to be diplomatic, keep things professional. That was fine with her. She didn't need his pity. "Look, the other night was fun, but it had nothing to do with this place, right? We had fun. We both got what we wanted. Now we forget about it and move on."

"You can't seriously expect me to act like it never happened." Cole's words were carefully measured, his playful smile nowhere to be seen.

If she didn't know better, she would have thought he was offended. His words flowed like silk, but his gray eyes held a different emotion as he pinned her with his gaze. Was she imagining it or did he look... disappointed?

Shifting in her seat, she tried to quell her own warring emotions.

They needed to be able to work together, at least until she could figure things out. And despite her racing pulse, she didn't want him to know how hard this was for her. She wouldn't give him the satisfaction. Was it her fault she couldn't look at him without her blood pressure spiking? Or that she couldn't stop thinking about the smoking hot kisses he'd lavished upon her body?

"And it would be so easy for you to forget?" he challenged with a knowing grin, forcing her to remember the feel of his sinful hands claiming her body and the way he'd made her come over and over again.

Damn him!

"Yes," she lied, struggling to keep her tone light.

She stood and moved to the window. It was a desperate attempt to put more space between them. The room had grown insufferably hot, a fact that had little to do with the temperature and a lot to do with the way his gaze lingered on her mouth, like he was imagining all the dirty things she could do with it.

Only he didn't have to imagine, did he? He had firsthand knowledge.

"Olivia."

She froze at the feel of his breath on her neck.

With the protection of the desk gone, she was defenseless. His hand snaked around her waist, crushing her body to his. He leaned in, his breath hot on her cheek as he pressed her body to the cool glass of the window with his massive weight. His arousal found the swell of her ass and she melted against the hard muscles of his chest, an unexpected gasp escaping her lips as desire ripped through her.

It was all the invitation he needed.

He turned her to face him, tipping her chin toward his lips. His mouth descended upon hers without hesitation, his tongue savagely forcing her lips apart. The five o'clock shadow she found so sexy scratched the tender flesh of her face once again, marking her. It was a deep kiss, the kind of sensual exploration she'd craved her whole life. The feel of his tongue sliding over hers, probing and thrusting, left her yearning as she rotated her hips, angling for a deeper connection. The cool glass at her back did little to regulate her temperature as Cole lifted her skirt, his hand sliding up her thigh with the promise of explosive pleasure.

She whimpered with anticipation when his hand reached the top of her leg and shifted. His palm pressed to her center with just enough pressure to send her body into overdrive. Unable to stop herself, she rotated her hips again, savoring the friction their joining created. The divine sensation did little to satisfy the growing need between her legs.

If anything, it ignited a fresh torrent of desire even greater than the last, tearing through her body like wildfire.

When he delved inside her panties and stroked her slick flesh, Olivia was sure she'd lose her mind.

Hell, she'd give away her sanity freely for just one more sinful stroke.

The sentiment must've been written all over her face because he quickly obliged, trailing a skilled finger down her center and sinking it deep inside her. She moaned with pleasure and was rewarded with another. Her body tightened around him, tensing for release with each thrust of his hand.

His mouth angled over hers, muting the sounds of her breathless cries. Spiraling toward climax, she clutched the soft fabric of his jacket, anchoring herself in the moment. He used his weight to pin her pulsating hips to the window and slipped his fingers deeper, hooking them toward the spot that was sure to send her soaring.

"You feel so fucking good," he groaned, a deft hand slipping from her neck to find the hardened nipple of her breast. "I want to make you come so hard you'll never forget it."

Shit. Panic seized her.

What was she doing? What were they doing?

The whole point of this discussion was to forget about sex with Cole, not fall into his arms again with the promise of an unforgettable orgasm. An orgasm she was certain he could deliver if he put his mind to it.

"Stop," she panted, pushing him away and sucking in a deep breath. This man was practically her mortal enemy. She could not let him seduce her again. Correction. She didn't *want* him to. "We can't do this."

"Why not?" he asked, flashing her that wicked grin. "As you so smartly pointed out, we're both adults."

"I'm serious. Play time is over," she insisted, sidestepping out of his reach and straightening her skirt. "From here on out, it's all business."

Guilt tugged at her as frustration flashed in his eyes.

Whatever chemistry they had was irrelevant. He was no

longer a wild one-night fling. He was the boss, the man who'd *stolen* her freaking job. He'd just have to figure out how to keep it in his pants because this was one round he wasn't going to win. She might not have control of her future right now, but she could sure as hell control who she had sex with.

Cole scrubbed a hand over his face, as if trying to erase the memory of their hot and heavy make-out session from his mind.

"All right, *Sweetheart*. There is one more thing I could use your help with, then." His words were clipped, all business now. Relief filled her. She could handle business, preferred it in fact. If they never had to talk about *that* night again, she might just be able to do this. "I expect to be included in all strategy meetings and pitches moving forward, so I'll need complete files on your top ten accounts. I'd like them on my desk tomorrow morning."

Cole stood and stalked out of the room without a backward glance or another word.

His rigid shoulders spoke volumes though. He was definitely pissed off, although it hardly seemed fair. She was the one who would have to forgo a date with Mr. Bubble in order to meet his deadline, after all.

Hoping to find a stray bottle of Tylenol for her blossoming headache, she checked her drawer one more time.

No such luck. It was going to be a long night.

13

———

COLE

COLE OBSERVED SILENTLY as Olivia circled the room, eyeing each of her team members over the top of her glasses. She said nothing as their pens flew over the pages in front of them, furiously scribbling notes in their tablets. She had asked them to gather in the conference room for a brainstorming session, so here they sat, gathered around the table flexing their creative muscles.

In a few minutes they'd be vying for her approval and the opportunity to lead the Mama's Muffins advertising campaign. It was a unique approach, but he was more interested in the end result. He was anxious to see what they'd come up with for Mama's.

Better yet, the exercise gave him a chance to study Olivia in her element. She was basically ignoring him anyway, so he might as well look his fill while her attention was focused elsewhere.

Her brow wrinkled in concentration as she read over the shoulder of a Junior Associate.

Whatever the kid had written down, his chances of leading the campaign didn't look good.

When she leaned down and whispered in his ear, any sympathy Cole felt for the guy vanished.

If anyone got to feel her breath on their cheek, it should be him.

Of course, he'd prefer her panting in the throes of orgasm, but he was hardly in a position to be picky since she was doing her damnedest to pretend Friday night had never happened.

Try as he might, he couldn't figure her out. She was smart, gorgeous, hyper-driven, and unlike any woman he'd been with before. He was used to working with, and dating, shrewd women who flaunted their femininity and flexed every female wile they'd been given to get ahead. Only she wasn't like that. She seemed determined to downplay the physical aspects that might otherwise give her an advantage in the office.

Cole had been around the world of advertising a long time, and if there was one thing he knew for certain, it was that sex *sold*. It sold products, services, and campaigns. And yet Olivia did everything she could to neutralize the fact that she was a woman.

More power to her, he supposed. He respected her integrity, but that didn't mean it wasn't a mistake.

Today she wore a black suit with red accents and a pair of sensible black heels. Black was the single most boring color on the planet as far as he was concerned, but it worked for her, the tailored suit hugging her body in all the right places. Her hair was pulled back in a ponytail again and she wore minimal makeup.

Cole frowned. Was she *trying* to mask her beauty in blandness?

If so, she'd failed miserably.

With her delicate features, the natural look worked just as well as the black suit.

Of course, a little color in her cheeks would do wonders, and he knew just how to elicit that response, if only she'd let him.

As if sensing his thoughts, Olivia jerked her gaze up to meet his.

He smiled and received a tight-lipped frown in return.

"Time," she called, prompting several groans from the group. She tossed a black marker to the guy she'd been whispering to. "Jack, you take notes today."

Jack scrambled to the front of the conference room, nearly tripping over his own two feet. He pushed a crop of unruly blond hair from his eyes and prepared himself to jot down the ideas of his peers on the dry erase board mounted on the wall.

Cole couldn't decide if the kid was an overachieving kiss-ass or a genuinely awkward human being. With two left feet, a red bowtie, and wire rimmed glasses, the latter seemed like the obvious answer. There was no doubt Jack was smart. Pritchard wouldn't have hired him otherwise, but did he have the fire in his belly to do the job?

"All right, people, let's see what you've got," Olivia said.

"From our kitchen to yours, Mama's muffins are baked with love."

"Fresh from Mama's oven, you've never had a muffin this good."

"Mama's Muffins: because even mamas need a break sometimes."

"Got muffins?"

"Nothing says lovin' like Mama's Muffins."

"Who's your Mama?"

The ideas just kept coming, flowing like word-vomit, each one worse than the last.

Cole shook his head in disgust. He couldn't believe his ears. These were some of the most experienced and sought-after agents in the city, the finest Pritchard, Bennett, & Associates had to offer, and this was the best they could do?

Any minute they were bound to break out in Kumbaya and indulge in one big, happy, fucking love-fest.

It was nauseating.

"Keep them coming, people," Olivia encouraged, although Jack and his not-so-magic marker were struggling to keep up.

She scanned the room, passing Cole over once again.

He cleared his throat, refusing to be shut out any longer. He had a job to do, after all. One he suspected wasn't going to earn him any friends and would surely make him a few enemies. It wouldn't be the first time, but he hadn't gotten where he was today by worrying about what other people thought.

"If I may," he offered, rising from his chair and approaching Jack. He held out his hand for the marker and the kid froze, his gaze swinging wildly from Cole to Olivia. He hadn't encountered much wildlife in the city, but he was sure the panic on Jack's face was akin to a deer in the headlights. If this was all it took to rattle the guy, he had no business representing PBA. The kid looked like he wanted to curl up under the table in the fetal position. "Olivia?"

With a look of annoyance, she nodded her head, signaling Jack to relinquish the pen.

He returned to his seat at the table and Cole uncapped the marker, ceremoniously crossing out every suggestion the team had made.

And damn if it didn't feel good.

"Excuse me, what exactly are you doing?" Olivia asked, stalking to the front of the room where she stood toe-to-toe with him. Her blue eyes flashed and he could feel the tension emanating from her body.

Mission accomplished. He had her undivided attention now.

"We're starting fresh," he explained, a smirk hitching up the right corner of his mouth. "Pritchard, Bennett, & Associates owes the client our very best and this isn't it."

"With all due respect, my team and I have been working the Mama's Muffins account for years," she returned, a tight, fake smile plastered on her face, "and we understand their needs quite well."

"You're kidding, right?" He knew he was treading in dangerous territory, but he couldn't help himself. Seeing Olivia flushed and excited? He wanted more and he knew just how to get it. If she didn't want to talk about their night together, they could talk about her other favorite subject: work. "Nothing says lovin' like Mama's Muffins? If this is the best we can do, we should all pack our bags and get the hell out of New York."

The room fell silent. No one spoke. No one moved. He wasn't even sure they were still breathing. So be it. He could wait them out.

Besides, it was the most fun he'd had all day.

"All right, then." Olivia turned on her heel and retreated to the table where she perched on the end, legs crossed. "You've been on the account now for what, twenty minutes? Dazzle us with your insights."

Cole pocketed the marker, stripped off his jacket and rolled up his sleeves, taking his sweet-ass time as he collected his thoughts. "Mama's is a New York icon and like New York, Mama's should be edgy, slick, and sexy."

"Those muffins are about as sexy as my nana riding bareback," Olivia quipped, drawing a few snickers from her team.

So they were still alive after all.

She crossed her arms over her chest, looking pleased with herself.

"Maybe that's the problem," he returned, feigning confusion. She was going to take the hard road, he realized. It didn't matter what he suggested, she was predisposed to disagreeing. *So much for starting fresh.* Well, if she wanted to do things the hard way that was fine by him. He'd never backed down from a fight in his life and he wasn't about to start now. Not even when facing a pissed-off blonde with a vendetta. "How many New Yorkers do you know that aspire to a frumpy, muffin-induced carb coma?"

Olivia shook her head. "Doesn't matter. Mama will never go for it."

"We'll never know if we don't try." He reached around Olivia and grabbed a file off the table. She flinched instinctively, leaning away as he invaded her space. It didn't matter. The scent of her perfume, a light floral blend, filled his nostrils and nearly derailed his focus as he recalled the last time he'd been this close to her. "According to the notes I have, her family is moving into position to take control of the company. It may not be Mama making the decision this time."

"Regardless, it's extremely risky. You're talking about sexing up their *family* business." She emphasized the word family as if a jackass like him couldn't possibly grasp the concept. "We need to stick with what works."

Doing his best to let the sting of her potshot roll off his back, he stretched and yawned. She really didn't know anything about him and now wasn't the time to let his personal feelings get the best of him.

"*Bor-ing!* The last time I checked, this was a city thriving with young working professionals, not the muffin-loving families of suburbanites. It's time for Mama's to get with the millennium."

"It's not going to happen," she argued, shaking her head.

"Not with an attitude like that," he shot back. Damn, she was stubborn. He scanned the room, searching for a nonexistent ally. "Are you all really so afraid to try something new? Because I'm here to cure you of that fear."

Olivia tipped her head to the ceiling and took a deep breath.

He would have bet his partnership she was counting to ten in her head as she fought for composure. It was kind of cute how she got all flustered when she was angry.

"Hear me out," he suggested, trying a more diplomatic approach. He had to get Olivia on board if he was going to stand a chance with her team, and right now not a single one of them was willing to even make eye contact. "Mama's got a muffin for every occasion...you're fired, breakups, the morning after."

"Genius." Olivia slid off the table. She circled Cole as though she smelled blood in the water, her lips curled back in a devious smile. "Maybe Mama can even add some new muffins to the menu. Let's see. How about 'It's Not Me, It's You', the 'Coyote Ugly', and maybe a 'Trump' for good measure? They'll be all the rage."

Nervous laughter filled the room.

Her team sat idly in the crossfire, enjoying the show, but he wasn't going to rise to the bait. He'd never allowed his emotions to rule him in the boardroom and he wasn't about to start now. Besides, if he was honest with himself, he kind of liked this fiery side of Olivia. She brought the same passion to the office she brought to the bedroom.

Pritchard had been dead on in his assessment of her: smart as a whip with a tongue twice as sharp. He liked how she wasn't afraid to challenge him. Still, that didn't mean he was going to allow her to push him around.

He had a reputation to uphold.

"Cute, Olivia, but I'm serious. We need a fresh angle."

"That may be," she snickered, "but I don't think morning-after muffins are what Mama had in mind when she asked us to begin working on a new campaign."

"Do you have a better suggestion?" He smiled, revealing the dimple that had helped him win more arguments than he could count. "Because I'm telling you Mama's needs an edge and we are going to give it to them."

"Mama's is my account, and I'll make that decision," she challenged, daring him to disagree. Realizing he'd pushed her too hard already, he remained silent. The tension in her shoulders, the angry tilt of her head, and the frustration in her eyes said it all. Now wasn't the time to pull rank on her. She'd stood her ground, gone head-to-head with him, but she was clearly feeling raw about the whole thing. "Let's call it quits for today, everyone. We can regroup tomorrow, but keep brainstorming. It's time to show Mr. Bennett what we're made of."

14

OLIVIA

OLIVIA CRAMMED her notes in the Mama's Muffins file, hoping to make a hasty exit on the heels of the Junior Associates, who were rapidly funneling into the hall. The last thing she wanted was to be left alone with Cole, the cocky, arrogant jerk-face who seemed hell-bent on torturing her.

Who did he think he was bashing her team like that anyway?

She wouldn't stand for it. Her team worked hard, and they deserved respect. She slammed the file closed and clutched it to her chest as she headed for the door. She could think of one or two places he could stick his new angle.

"Olivia?" Cole's words cut through the silence, freezing her in her tracks. Halfway to the door, but no escape in sight. "Do you have a few minutes? I'd like to speak with you."

She considered lying. She could tell him she had another meeting, but what would be the point? He'd just hunt her down later. Better to face the music now and get it over with. No doubt he was pissed about the large dose of 'your ideas are shit-tastic' attitude she'd given him.

Not that he didn't deserve it.

He deserved all of that and more as far as she was concerned.

Still, it wasn't like her to go for the throat.

She prided herself on being levelheaded and professional, but Cole was just one of those people who pushed her bitch-buttons. She hardly knew the man, but there was all this *stuff* between them, and she just couldn't let it go.

Not yet anyway.

"Sure, I've got a few minutes," she conceded, glancing at her watch before returning to her seat at the head of the table. Dread settled in the pit of her stomach, but she flashed him the warmest smile she could muster given the circumstances.

"Is there a problem?" With narrowed eyes, he watched her intently and waited for the answer.

Even with that accusing stare and wrinkled brows, he was a handsome man, a fact Olivia silently cursed as she was reminded this was strictly business and this man had stolen her partnership.

"A problem?" she countered, shifting her face into a mask of confusion.

She could play the dumb blonde people expected her to be, just this once. It beat the hell out of telling him what she really thought, since the landlord wasn't likely to accept a pink slip for next month's rent.

"Let me put it another way." He dragged his fingers through his tousled hair, looking frustrated himself. She was reminded of the gentleness of those hands and the pleasure they'd given her. The very thought sent her traitorous pulse soaring. Why couldn't she just forget about that stupid dare? "I think you're letting your personal feelings for me color your judgment here."

"Excuse me?" Anger sparked low in her belly, threatening to explode in a slew of four-letter words that would make her own father blush. "My personal feelings for you? Are you really that much of a self-involved asshat?"

Cole shrugged, looking nonplussed. "What else am I supposed to think?"

Evidently he wasn't quite sure what to make of her childish name-calling, so he just ignored it altogether. Of course, Mr. Perfect was above that too.

Probably for the best, she thought, as she counted to ten, trying to get a grip on her temper.

"You know Mama's campaigns are stale and outdated, yet you refused to even listen to my ideas."

"Look, I get it. You're new here and you want to make a name for yourself, but I won't have you doing it at the expense of my team." She sighed and crossed her arms, unsure of why she was even arguing with him. He was being completely impossible. "Did it occur to you for even one minute that my team is the best in this office, and those brainstorming sessions are a critical factor in our success? Award-winning campaigns don't just drop out of the sky, you know. Like people, sometimes ideas have to be nurtured, molded, and crafted. Instead of tearing the team down, you could have helped me guide them in the right direction in a more collaborative fashion."

Cole studied her for an eternity before he finally responded. "Interesting."

"Interesting? That's all?" She arched her brow, unable to hide her disgust. "You insulted my team. Did you really think I was going to sit there and let you speak to them that way?"

Surprise washed over his face and she was horrified to realize that was *exactly* what he'd expected. So he'd heard the rumors and probably her nickname, too.

Ice Queen.

Maybe she'd earned it, maybe not.

Olivia knew she had a reputation for being tough, but above

all else, she was fair. She offered constructive criticism and expected her team to work hard, but she also shared the praise and she sure as hell didn't berate them publicly.

She took a deep breath. She didn't have the luxury of feeling sorry for herself right now.

So he saw her as the Ice Queen. That was beyond her control. Sure, it stung, but it didn't really matter.

This was business, after all.

"That may be how you run your company, but it's not how I run my team. I will not have my people humiliated for your entertainment. I've worked with these people a long time and I've earned the right to challenge them. You haven't."

"I'm a partner here," he reminded her, "which means I have every right. We owe our clients the best and that wasn't it. I won't apologize for pushing the team to be better, although I may have mishandled the situation today."

"You think?"

"It won't happen again, but I still intend to be very hands-on."

"Yes," she sneered, unable to cut off the snarky reply before it escaped her lips. "I believe we already established that fact."

"Excuse me?"

"Nothing," she recanted as common sense took root. What the hell was she thinking, antagonizing him like this? As a partner, he had Jonathan's ear and with it the ability to make or break her future. The last thing she needed was for him to think she was a jilted schoolgirl. "I apologize. I shouldn't have brought it up."

"No, if there's something on your mind, we should get it out in the open now," he reasoned, crossing his legs and leaning back in his chair, amusement lighting his gray eyes.

He looked completely relaxed, while Olivia herself felt like a bundle of nerves.

"What is there to talk about? You look like a guy who's had more than his fair share of one-night stands. You know how it works." A shaky laugh rolled off her lips. "But I guess it didn't quite go as planned this time, huh? I'm sure you never expected to see my shining face again."

"That's hardly fair!" he growled, rising from his chair and closing the gap between them in a few short strides.

He towered over her, looking both dangerous and sexy in that moment, raw emotion flashing in his eyes. She wasn't sure if he wanted to grab her by the shoulders and shake the shit out of her or if he wanted to do something a whole lot dirtier.

Judging by his ragged breath, her money was on door number two: down and dirty.

The thought of his lips pressed to hers had her hormones in a damn frenzy. Desire coiled in her belly, reaching out and planting some very delicious, very NC-17 thoughts in her mind as her gaze drifted from his full lips to further south. Her body reacted to his nearness as though it had a will of its own and she found herself craving his taste, her anger dissipating with each passing second.

Cole's hooded eyes and the erection he couldn't hide suggested he was fighting the same losing battle.

For the first time in her career, she wanted to be the girl who had sex in the supply closet and to hell with the consequences. The tension curling between them was a live, ravenous thing that threatened to suffocate her even as she resisted.

"You're the one who ran out," he whispered gruffly, breaking the silence. "You never even gave me a chance. Hell, I wanted to take you to dinner."

He'd wanted to see her again? Olivia's chest tightened at the revelation.

She reached for him, but stopped short. If she'd stayed that morning, would things be any different? She doubted it.

Cole wasn't the monogamous type. Neither was she.

Besides, he was the boss now. She didn't have the luxury of indulging in office romance.

All it would take was one person catching wind of her sleeping with the boss and any hope of promotion would go straight out the window. Or worse, if she *did* get a promotion, everyone would assume it was because she was screwing her boss.

Her very hot boss.

And besides, she couldn't forget it was his name on the door, not hers.

Maybe it wasn't his fault, but that didn't change the fact Pritchard had picked Cole over her. He'd blown into town and taken the one thing she so desperately needed and had given nothing in return.

"Really, Cole? What did you expect?" Olivia stood, forcing him to take a step back. She smoothed her face to a look of indifference and squashed the burning need to feel his touch. This was how it had to be. "It was pretty apparent you only had one night in mind."

"No," he argued, his eyes raging like storm clouds. "Don't you dare do that. Don't pretend you didn't feel it, too. You didn't leave your friend with the check and sidle up to that bar for good conversation."

Her cheeks flamed. She hadn't counted on him calling her out. "You were watching me?"

"Of course I was watching you," he retorted, his defenses melting into a crooked smile. "You were the most beautiful woman in the bar. Everyone was watching you."

A thrill raced through her veins, but she quickly tamped it down. Fair or not, he was her boss now. And regardless of whatever everyone else might think, she *didn't* sleep with her bosses.

"It doesn't matter. It's over now. It has to be. Do you have any idea what they say about women who get caught screwing the boss?"

"Sweetheart," he drawled, trailing a hand seductively down her arm, "what we do behind closed doors is no one's business but ours."

"You know," she stammered, hating the way her body reacted to his touch with fireworks and songbirds, "I kind of hate you sometimes."

"If that's code for 'I want to fuck you until I can't walk straight', then I kind of hate you, too."

Before she could protest, his lips were crashing against her mouth, claiming her and burning a trail of hungry kisses down her throat as he nipped at the sensitive flesh. His strong hands gripped her arms, pulling her flush against him, her aching breasts crushed to his solid chest. They were so close she could feel the heat rolling off his body.

She could bask in that heat all day, writhing in the pleasure he offered.

When Cole's hands dropped to her ass, cupping the cheeks and slamming her hips into him —*hard* —she liked it. Liked feeling his erection pressed against her belly in search of her wet heat. And god was she wet. He could bring her from zero to orgasm in a heartbeat. Nerves were firing all over her body, a frenzy she fully expected to result in earth-shattering, orgasmic satisfaction.

Unable to stop herself, she rolled her hips toward him, seeking relief for the pressure building between her legs as the dampness in her panties spread.

Thinking only of the screaming need searing through her body, she grabbed his tie and pulled him close, ravaging his lips with desperate need. He growled in response and spun her around so her backside was pressed firmly against his erection. Her pulse spiked, bringing desire with it.

His intentions were clear.

She leaned forward, putting her breasts to the table, and rubbed her ass against his hard ridge, enjoying the very exquisite, very male feel of him. With no time to waste, he hitched up her skirt, the chill of the cool office air washing over her rear. He exposed her bare flesh, running a hand gently over her right cheek, before giving it a firm slap. The sting heightened her excitement and she wriggled with anticipation.

They were silent except for the sound of his zipper sliding down, freeing the erection that would satisfy her raging hormones. He dragged the tip of his cock down the cleft of her ass, sending a thrill up her spine.

Finally. He was positioned to take her.

A sharp knock at the door yanked Olivia back to reality.

Holy hell! Had she lost her freaking mind?

She separated herself from Cole and flung herself into one of the empty chairs that surrounded the table milliseconds before Jack opened the door and stuck his head in. She glanced at Cole, relieved to see he'd positioned himself behind one of the high-backed chairs, effectively masking his open trousers.

"Uh, Mr. Pritchard needs to see you, Mr. Bennett."

The look in Cole's eyes was deadly as he turned to the Junior Associate. "I'll be right there."

Honestly, it was a wonder Jack didn't pee his pants, she thought, a nervous laugh rolling off her lips as he backed out of the room.

Had Jack seen them going at it like two horny teenagers? She hoped to god not. Which reminded her of what she had to do.

Olivia took a deep breath and braced herself for the fallout.

"Look, it was a dare, okay?" she blurted out. "Nothing more.

If it hadn't been you, it would have been somebody else in that bar."

Shock registered on Cole's face, followed by denial.

She couldn't blame him. It did seem pretty tasteless in retrospect.

"A fucking dare, huh?" The smile that twisted his lips was anything but pleased. "Sweetheart, it may have started that way, but in case you haven't noticed, we can't be in the same room without ripping each other's clothes off, so why keep fighting it?"

Her pride wanted her to deny the crap out of his statement, but what would be the point? Her breathless state spoke louder than any argument she could form.

She shrugged. "I like sex as much as the next girl. I had an itch that needed scratching, so I scratched it. It didn't really matter who it was with."

"I don't believe you."

"Believe it or don't. It doesn't change the facts." Olivia's stomach turned at the heartless words. Shit, she was earning that Ice Queen reputation right now. "We're both adults. We have to work together, and if you like your cushy new job, you'll keep your hands—and your penis—to yourself. I will *not* jeopardize my career, or my reputation, for meaningless sex. No matter how good it is. You shouldn't either."

She moved toward the door, desperate to escape the confines of the stifling room and Cole's accusing stare before it consumed her. Like the wild Kudzu vine of the south, he had a way of overpowering everyone and everything in his path and Olivia wasn't sure she had the strength to hold her ground.

She wasn't even sure she wanted to.

As she twisted the knob to freedom, he delivered a parting shot.

"I don't believe you. The way you cried my name? That was more than just a dare."

15

COLE

CCole drummed his fingers on the table, fuming. He was due in Pritchard's office, but he was too pissed to go anywhere just yet. Better to be a few minutes late and get his temper under control first given the way Olivia had just nuked him.

He wasn't buying that 'dare' bullshit for a second.

Maybe it had started out that way, but either she was a hell of an actress, or she was in denial.

He was betting on denial.

Maybe Olivia could fool herself, but she wasn't fooling him.

The way she'd reacted to his touch? That wasn't just convenience. That was authentic. She had enjoyed every moment in that hotel room—and every stolen moment since—just as he had.

Maybe even more.

No, their problem wasn't sex; it was his partnership with Pritchard.

She was never going to forgive him for that one, despite the fact that it was entirely out of his control.

And maybe he had been a bit tough on her team today, but he stood by the message. *Nothing says lovin' like Mama's Muffins?*

He couldn't have come up with a more cliché tag line if he tried. No way in hell were they pitching that garbage as long as his name was on the door.

Shit. Cole rubbed his hands across his face and groaned.

He'd completely screwed up again, leading with his ego instead of his brain.

Instead of showing Olivia she was a valuable asset to PBA, he'd managed to completely alienate her in front of her team like the self-involved asshat she accused him of being.

So much for earning her trust.

Truth was, hearing her say they should forget that first night together had really burned, and he'd let that frustration affect his behavior today. Cole, who'd built a reputation for being cool and collected, had lost his temper and let his personal feelings bleed over to his professional life.

Olivia was right. Instead of tearing the group down, he should have helped her build them up. And today's screw-up had probably put him another two steps back with her and the team.

He headed to Pritchard's office.

Halfway there, his cell vibrated, demanding his attention.

He reached into his pocket to retrieve the phone and glanced at the caller ID. He didn't particularly feel like chatting with Brody, but the guy usually only called when he had information, and his connections were one of the assets he brought to PBA. Now wasn't the time to start ignoring them, no matter how black his mood.

He swiped accept. "Cole Bennett."

"Hey, man," Brody practically shouted through the phone. Probably to ensure he'd be heard over the background noise. Cole would've bet his paycheck Brody was at happy hour. "Long time no talk."

"Yeah, I've been a little busy with the move," Cole confirmed, not bothering to elaborate.

"No worries," Brody returned. "I won't keep you long, but I heard something interesting today and I thought you'd want to hear it sooner rather than later."

"I'm listening."

"McKenzie lost one of their top clients today, Vixen Enterprises."

"The lingerie company?" Cole asked.

"Yeah, man. Can you believe it? Talk about a golden goose."

"How reliable is this information?"

"Let's just say I'm sitting across the table from a very drunk, very unemployed young woman from McKenzie who used to work on the account. I hear there will be a formal announcement tomorrow, but Vixen is going to be in the market for a new agency."

Cole rolled his eyes. Leave it to Brody to try and take advantage of the situation in more ways than one. As usual, the guy oozed class.

Tamping down his disgust, he thanked Brody for the tip and disconnected.

He did a quick search on Vixen Enterprises as he walked to Pritchard's office. The results confirmed what he suspected. Vixen was a giant, holding a majority share of the U.S.'s more than $13 billion in annual lingerie sales. Landing the account would be huge not only for the agency that landed the account, but also the individual who made the pitch. It would be a career-maker for some lucky bastard.

As he processed this information, an idea began to take shape. He knocked on Pritchard's door, determined to see it through.

He found his partner hunched behind his desk, poring over the latest edition of Ad Week.

"You wanted to see me?"

"Yeah," Pritchard confirmed, checking his watch. "But I need to make this quick. The wife made dinner plans at some posh new restaurant in Midtown and she'll have my balls if I'm late."

Cole shook his head and laughed. "Fair enough."

Pritchard's face shifted, a frown tugging at his thin mouth. "What the hell happened in the Mama's Muffins meeting today?"

Shit. Apparently news travelled fast at PBA. Stalling for time, he gave his partner a placating smile. "Jonathan—"

"Don't you Jonathan me," Pritchard returned, shaking his head. "I don't know how they did things in England, but here we're a team! You ever pull a stunt like that again, you'll be out on your ass faster than you can say null and void. You may have brought an impressive client list, but I guarantee you my lawyers are better."

Cole fought to keep his face blank, not wanting Pritchard to see how affected he was by the threat. Another failed business venture? Not an option. He'd busted his ass to get where he was today, and he was going to make damn sure his time at PBA was a success.

Still, there was no denying he'd fucked up with Olivia.

"Understood. I pushed the team a little too hard today. I was trying to feel them out and it backfired. Lesson learned. You can rest assured it won't happen again."

Pritchard gave a curt nod, seemingly satisfied. "Good."

Cole studied his partner, assessing his mood and determining the right approach.

He'd need to tread lightly, using the power of suggestion to steer him in the desired direction. "Before you go, there is something else we need to discuss."

"Oh?"

"I'll get right to the point. McKenzie lost their bread and

butter. Vixen Enterprises is going to be in the market for a new agency."

"You're sure?" Pritchard asked, his brows furrowed.

"They'll be making a formal announcement tomorrow."

Pritchard drummed his fingers on the desk. "Vixen is a cash cow. And securing that contract would bring a lot of other lucrative projects to the agency. We'll need our best on this."

"Agreed, which is why I want Olivia on this project. She's sharp, driven, and let's be honest, you and I don't know shit about lingerie."

Plus, if they landed the Vixen account, Olivia's career would skyrocket.

He couldn't give her back the partnership he'd taken, but this would be the next best thing, and maybe, just maybe, it would make up for everything that had happened between them.

"This is too big for an Associate to pitch alone, even one as experienced as Olivia." Pritchard tented his fingers, a sure sign he was thinking through the implications of the project. "I want you on this pitch with her, so you'd damn well better figure out how to get along without killing one another. I don't want a repeat of today's little show."

Cole nodded but said nothing. Jonathan didn't need more platitudes. He needed results.

Results he and Olivia would deliver.

"Pull whatever resources you need. Vixen is now our top priority."

Cole returned to his office, prepared to pull an all-nighter and unable to shake thoughts of Olivia. Working the Vixen pitch with her over the next couple of weeks was going to be a blessing and a curse. Not to mention the ultimate test of his self-control.

The long hours would afford him the opportunity to get

closer to her, and, if he was lucky, circumvent some of those walls she'd built around herself.

On the other hand, he had no doubt she'd be resistant and would fight their chemistry as long as they were working together.

And since neither of them was going anywhere any time soon, maybe that was for the best.

He had too much invested in the partnership with Pritchard to let things go south. He was committed to New York. Hell, he'd even made an offer on an apartment with a view of Central Park.

Common sense told him he needed to put his cock on probation when it came to Olivia, but he wasn't ready to give up yet. They were consenting adults with off-the-charts chemistry and he was determined to find a way to mix business and pleasure, if only he could convince her to give him the chance.

16

———

OLIVIA

A MESSAGE BLINKED on Olivia's screen, and for the second time that morning, she broke out in a cold sweat.

Shit. Cole wanted to see her in his office.

Now.

She'd hoped to avoid him for the next couple of days, so she could...what? Wallow in private all weekend and face him again on Monday?

Olivia silently cursed her quasi self-control.

The hot/cold thing between her and Cole was getting old, and she felt doubly guilty for sending him mixed messages.

Still, the idea of facing him after the night before was excruciating.

Despite her cold words, he'd have to be an idiot not to sense her desire. The tension between them was nearly tangible and it didn't look like it would be dissipating any time soon. If anything, their mutual frustration seemed to be fueling the fire. If they could just separate the sex from work it would be fine, she reasoned, but that wasn't an option.

Add the fact the office was abuzz with rumors of their fight and, according to Chloe, the words 'sexual tension' had been mentioned once or twice, and yeah, she'd never been so happy it was Friday in her life.

At least no one knew what had really happened behind that closed door. Pritchard would have her ass if he found out.

She shifted uncomfortably in her seat as the feeling of déjà vu overwhelmed her. Whatever Cole wanted, it didn't sound good, but hiding in her office like a coward wasn't going to make it any better.

Olivia trudged to Cole's office, bypassing his admin entirely.

It wasn't like she needed to be announced. Cole had asked to see her and she could see him waiting behind his monstrous desk even before stepping foot in the office. Fear blossomed in her stomach as she padded across the plush carpet.

Halfway there, she realized he was on the phone.

"Have a seat," he mouthed, motioning to the empty chairs before returning his attention the person on the other end of the line.

Typical. Had he called her in here just to remind her who was in charge?

She cut her eyes at him, red-hot anger bubbling up from her belly.

Taking a deep breath, she lowered herself into the seat across from him and crossed her arms. Getting angry with Cole usually ended with blistering hot kisses and while she didn't know what she was doing in his office, she did know those lips were off limits.

For her, anyway.

"Anna, we've been through this," he said, shaking his head, a wide grin on his face. "It's not a big deal. The closing is next week." He laughed. "You're relentless, you know that, right?"

Who the hell was Anna? Olivia had never seen Cole so relaxed in all the time she'd known him. Whoever she was, they must be close.

Not that she cared.

"Look, I've got to go. I have someone in my office. I'll talk to you later, okay?"

He hung up the phone and turned that panty-melting smile on her, causing her blood pressure to creep up.

Olivia wiped her sweaty palms on her thighs.

"Sorry about that. My sister," he explained. "Anyway, I'm sure you're wondering why I called you into my office."

Olivia nodded, still processing the idea that Cole had a sister. One he was apparently pretty close to. Who'd have guessed?

She didn't have long to dwell on it.

"I have a special project for you." He folded his hands on the desk, dragging the moment out endlessly. Masochist. "We just received word Vixen Enterprises is in the market for a new agency."

"They fired McKenzie?" She didn't believe it. The two companies had been in bed together for, well, forever. If it was true, every agency in town would be vying for the Vixen account. It was a multi-million-dollar contract. "Are you sure?"

"We have it on good authority that it will be a sudden death scenario. Each agency will get one shot, and one shot only, at the account. Winner takes all. We have three weeks to prepare."

"Three weeks?" Olivia scoffed. Impossible. Three weeks wasn't nearly enough time to come up with a worthy campaign. It couldn't be done.

"Three weeks, for three years," he confirmed. "I don't care what it takes, we are going to land that account. We need our best on this pitch, which is why I want you to lead the team with me. We'll be working together closely on this one."

She was too stunned to reply.

Leading a team with Cole? No way. The very idea was ridiculous. It had all the makings of a disaster.

Hell, they'd probably kill each other.

On the other hand, it was an opportunity. A big one. One she couldn't turn down.

And he knew it.

"Reassign everything you can to the Junior Associates. I don't care what else you're working on. Dump it," Cole ordered, pounding the desk to drive his point home. "It's time some of these people started pulling their weight around here. You can't do everything."

"Consider it done. I'll send out the new assignments today." Rising to her feet, Olivia retreated to the door. She might be a control freak, but she wasn't stupid. If they could secure the Vixen account, it would give her tremendous leverage with Pritchard and maybe another shot at a partnership. For that, she'd offload her other clients, but it didn't mean she was going to be led around by the nose while Cole pressed his advantage. "I just hope your idea of working together closely doesn't include fucking, because that's still off the table as far as I'm concerned."

She turned on her heel and left.

17

COLE

Cole followed Olivia back to her office. They didn't speak, but he was okay with that. There was plenty to occupy his mind and the view from behind wasn't so bad.

Hell, he didn't think he'd ever get tired of looking at her backside.

She hurried down the hall, her tight ass wiggling all the way as she typed on her phone.

It was no surprise when she crashed into the mail cart turning the corner, sending letters skittering to the floor. She stumbled back and Cole caught her by the elbow, preventing any serious damage.

"So sorry," she apologized to the kid pushing the cart.

Tucking her phone in the pocket of her blazer, she stooped to help pick up the mess. She shot Cole a dark look.

Now it was his fault she couldn't walk and type?

Standing, she deposited the mail on the cart. "Thanks," she finally grumbled, stepping into her office and doing her best to dismiss him.

Yeah, that wasn't happening.

Not after that little gem she'd delivered on her way out the door.

"My pleasure." He smiled and followed her into the tiny office, closing the door behind them. It was time to clear the air once and for all. The world was un-*fucking*-fair, a fact he knew as well as anyone, but if she couldn't put her anger aside, they'd never be able to work together, let alone secure the Vixen account. They needed to be in sync moving forward, which meant less attitude and more collaboration. "Do you have a few minutes? There are some things I'd like to discuss with you."

"What did you want to discuss?" she asked, straightening her back and smoothing her hair. With only inches separating them, it was impossible to ignore the intoxicating scent of her perfume. Or the unspoken arousal that filled the space between them. "Was it your three-step plan to ruin my career? Is Pritchard going to fire me if we can't play nice? Is that what's next, Cole? No doubt you have something really special planned for the grand finale."

"I think you're being a bit dramatic, don't you?" He tucked his hands in his pockets.

Did she really think her job was on the line? Pritchard was a total softy under that crotchety exterior. No one was getting fired. Mama's would end up with a better campaign than they expected and even if PBA didn't land the Vixen account, they'd make a hell of a bid for it with him and Olivia leading the team.

"Dramatic? You haven't seen dramatic yet." She cocked her hip and raised her chin defiantly. "Look, I get it. You've got loads of money and this is all one big friggin' laugh to you, but what we do here is important to me. I will not let one night of poor judgment ruin five years of hard work."

He wasn't sure what bugged him more, her assumption that he wasn't serious about his business, or her determination to downplay their night together.

"Like it or not, you're stuck with me on this one. We need to find a way to work together. Preferably without killing one another."

"You're right," she responded, through clenched teeth. "I don't like it, but I'll do my job without berating the people around me because I'm a team player. Think you can do the same?"

Cole fought to keep his face impassive. While her words stung, she wasn't wrong.

Hell, he deserved everything she threw at him and more.

He rubbed the back of his neck. "This isn't easy for me to say, but I fucked up with your team yesterday. I am sorry and it won't happen again."

Olivia pursed her lips.

Of course she wasn't going to let him off that easily.

"I asked Pritchard to put you on this bid because you're the best we've got." Her cheeks reddened at the compliment. He wasn't sure if it was embarrassment or guilt, but whatever it was, it seemed to soften her mood. "I fully expect us to work on this campaign as equals."

"Equals?" She studied his face as if seeing him for the first time.

What did she see when she looked at him?

He shoved the thought aside. It didn't matter. He knew what he saw when he looked at her, and right now he saw a woman on the edge, ready to lose control. Only a blind man would have missed the way her bottom lip quivered or the way she swallowed, as if fortifying her resolve.

Ignoring his better judgment, he leaned into her, stopping only when the peaks of her breasts brushed his chest. His balls tightened at the contact, anxious to finish what they'd started the day before. He brushed his fingers over her jawline, tipping her mouth to his.

It had only been a day, but it felt like an eternity since he'd tasted those sweet lips.

And like an addict, he needed that fix. Craved it. Couldn't think straight without it.

His eyes locked on Olivia, confirming her need matched his own.

Her breath hitched, but for once she didn't resist.

He moved slowly, skimming his lips over the corners of her mouth, teasing her and savoring the sweet taste of peppermint that clung to her lips.

The whimper that followed stroked more than his ego, bringing them closer, her body melting against him. When her lips found his, it was a languid kiss, unhurried and unlike any they'd shared before. She sucked on his bottom lip, nearly driving him mad, before delving into his mouth and caressing his tongue with her own.

When she finally pulled away, he was hard as a rock.

If her intention had been to leave him wanting more, she'd succeeded.

He adjusted his cock, knowing full well his erection would be visible to anyone who dared look.

"So, equals?" she asked again, as if the hard-on-inducing kiss had been a figment of his imagination.

How the hell she managed to do that, he'd never know.

"Always."

She sighed and yanked the door open. "Let me work on the reassignments this morning and we can meet up after lunch to talk strategy."

"Works for me," he agreed, stepping through the open door.

Their shoulders brushed as he squeezed by.

He wanted to tease her, tell her it was a 'no touching zone', but the guarded look she wore told him to bite his tongue and let the moment pass. Antagonizing her after the kiss they'd just shared wasn't going to earn her trust...or get her back in his bed.

18

COLE

COLE WATCHED as Olivia propped a small compact up on her desk and leaned down to check her makeup, completely oblivious to his presence in her doorway. She looked good to him, given the late hour, but what the hell did he know about makeup?

It was after six, and most of the office had cleared out already, but it was no surprise she was one of the few who'd stuck around.

He watched as she expertly applied a swipe of bright pink to her luscious bottom lip.

By the time she'd finished, he was already starting to get ideas about how he might rub that color off. She didn't need it anyway. She was a natural beauty. He hadn't known many, but there was no doubt Olivia was one of them. His cock stirred at the thought of touching her silky skin and he decided that interrupting beat the hell of standing there like a voyeur, given his wayward thoughts.

The last thing he needed was for her to find him lurking.

He knocked on the door lightly to draw her attention.

"Yes?" she said, pausing her routine for a moment.

When she looked up to see him filling her doorway, surprise flashed across her face before she returned to the task at hand. When she was done with the top lip, she swept all of the makeup into her bag and turned her attention to him.

"Sorry to interrupt," he offered, shifting his weight and stuffing his hands in his pockets.

He was used to seeing women in various stages of undress, but this? Not so much.

It was weirdly...intimate.

"What can I do for you, Cole?"

She'd used his name, and while her tone wasn't especially warm, it wasn't cold either. He'd take it. If he could avoid dangerous subjects, he might just be able to pull this off.

He hoped getting her out of the office might help repair the damage to their professional relationship and mend some of the bridges they'd burned without regard.

Despite their undeniable chemistry, there were still some hurt feelings lingering between them, and he was determined to make things right, one way or another.

Their afternoon meeting had gone all right, if you considered bickering like five-year-olds a success–which he did, given there was no bloodshed–but with the Vixen pitch on their plates, they needed to officially clear the air.

"I thought perhaps we could grab dinner and go over the details of the Vixen pitch before tomorrow's meeting with the rest of the team?" he offered.

When the idea had originally come to him, he was surprised to realize that having dinner with her, despite all of their bickering, was still appealing. It had been a while since he'd taken a woman to dinner—for business or pleasure.

"No need to worry," she responded, crossing her arms. "I'm ready for the meeting."

"I'm sure you are, but it will give us a chance to do some top-level brainstorming," he coaxed, hoping to persuade her. "Besides, even you need to eat."

"You're right. I do need to eat," she agreed.

"Perfect. I know a great—"

"Which is why I made plans," she finished without a trace of regret. "I have a date, so unfortunately, I'm already booked this evening."

"A date?" he asked, unable to the keep irritation from creeping into his voice. He couldn't believe it. Since when did Olivia go on dates? Weeknight dates, nonetheless. It was counter to everything he knew about her. She wanted to be a partner and she was going out to dinner with some asshole the night before they kicked off the biggest pitch of her life? "Sorry, I'm just a little surprised, given the magnitude of the Vixen account."

"Is it a problem?" she asked, leveling him with her blue eyes. A thin smile spread across her lips and he knew he'd stepped in it again. "Last time I checked, business hours were eight to five and I was your top closer."

"I didn't mean—"

"Like I said, I'm prepared."

Damn. He'd done it again. How he always managed to say the wrong thing and put her on the defensive was beyond him. Was he really such a condescending prick?

He'd never had so much trouble talking to a woman in all his life.

Come to think of it, he'd never had so much trouble understanding one, either.

Deep down, he knew the Vixen pitch was just an excuse to get her to agree to dinner with him. He'd considered she might say no, was even prepared for it. He'd never considered that she might actually have other plans.

Or that those plans might include another man.

Not that he was jealous. Cole Bennett didn't do jealous.

Besides, he wasn't exactly relationship material, so maybe it was best she was moving on. It would certainly simplify things around the office, assuming the sexual attraction between them fizzled out.

Who was he kidding? It didn't matter if another guy came sniffing around, he'd still want her. It wasn't like they needed to be exclusive, anyway. But his need to devour every inch of Olivia's delicious body hadn't faded.

If anything, it had grown stronger.

Being trapped in the same office together five days a week was going to be torture.

Everything about her provided temptation, from the long lines of her neck, to the sway of her hips, and even the way she wore her hair pulled up with those black schoolteacher glasses. He'd often wondered if she had any idea she looked like every teenage boy's fantasy. And given the fact that she suddenly seemed impervious to his charm, the whole situation was one big exercise in frustration.

"Was there something else?" she asked, slipping into a light coat the same shade of cerulean blue as her eyes.

He wanted to tell her the coat brought out the color in her eyes or she looked beautiful. He wanted to tell her to blow off her date and give him a chance to make things up to her. He even wanted to tell her to have fun and enjoy her night off. She certainly deserved it.

Instead he said, "Don't be late tomorrow. We've got a big day."

19

OLIVIA

Olivia stabbed a piece of broccoli with her fork and aimlessly pushed it around the edge of her plate. The thin white dish balanced precariously on her knees. One wrong move and she'd be scrubbing soy sauce out of the couch for the rest of her life. Chinese takeout had seemed like such a good idea when she'd called in the order, but now that she was eating it, the food felt more like an oily stone settling in her belly.

She was too keyed up to eat.

What she really needed was a trip to the gym to burn off some nervous energy and exhaust her overactive brain, but that was out of the question.

If she went to the gym, she'd have to face Chloe, and then Chloe would know she'd nearly had sex with Cole. Again.

Chloe had a sense about things like that and she knew there was no way she'd be able to hold out. She would ferret the truth out of Olivia and then she'd never hear the end of it.

Besides, admitting she'd almost had sex with Cole—*again*—would make the whole thing more real somehow, and she was perfectly happy basking in the state of denial. Denial was a pretty sweet gig. Denial meant a quiet night curled up in her favorite sweats with a YA romance and a bottle of wine.

She hadn't exactly lied when she'd told Cole she had plans, even if it wasn't really a date.

He didn't need to know it had been Chloe's latest attempt to set her up.

Or that against her better judgment, she'd agreed to have a drink with Alex, one of Chloe's friends, in a futile effort to erase the stupid dare from her memory. Or that she'd bailed on that, too, and had now curled up in a ball of worn-out sweats and sexual frustration.

"It doesn't get much better than this," she reasoned, dumping the still full plate on the coffee table and grabbing her Kindle.

She snuggled down into the worn couch cushions, waiting for the screen to come to life. Her pulse fluttered in anticipation. There was nothing more invigorating than the promise of young love and heart-stopping first kisses.

Olivia's book addiction was her one truly guilty pleasure.

Some women had shoes, others had jewelry. She had YA lit. Outside of work, reading was the only hobby she consistently made time to indulge. She could skip the gym, cleaning the bathroom, and even a full night's sleep for a swoon-worthy romance.

God knows she wasn't getting it in real life.

Well, unless you counted Cole. Which she didn't.

Besides, that wasn't romance. It was lust. Just sex. Totally meaningless. And totally over.

Definitely over.

Cole was off limits in a big way.

Maybe he could afford to be the playboy boss, but she couldn't afford to be just another conquest. There was just way too much potential for disaster in that. And he was an asshat, anyway.

Too bad she couldn't stop thinking about him. His eyes. His smile. His hands.

Oh, god. *Those hands.*

"No, no, no," she groaned.

Why was her brain torturing her like this, tempting her with things she could never have? It was masochistic.

She had to forget about Cole. As long as she was working for him, they had no future. At least, not one that didn't involve giving up everything she'd worked so hard for at PBA.

And she would be damned before she'd quit.

One way or another, she was going to get that promotion.

All her life, people had been telling her who she was, and what she could and couldn't do. She hadn't listened before, and she wasn't about to start now. Hell, those doubters were half the reason she'd moved to the city in the first place. Their doubt fueled her determination and her drive.

And she'd proven them wrong at every turn.

She wasn't about to give that up. Not for Cole Bennett. Not for anyone.

She needed to stick to the plan. It had gotten her this far, hadn't it?

She mindlessly turned the page on her e-reader. Her eyes skimmed over the words, but they didn't sink in. After rereading the same paragraph three times, she gave up entirely. Although she'd been counting down the days until the release of the last book in the trilogy, her head wasn't in it tonight.

Stellar. Now Cole was screwing with her reading time too.

Olivia stood and stretched. She grabbed her plate and carried it into the kitchen where she scraped the uneaten and congealed blob of food into the sink. It fell into the stainless-steel basin with an unimpressive splat that turned her stomach.

She rinsed the plate off and hit the switch for the garbage disposal. While it whirred the blob into oblivion, she refilled her wine glass. She flipped the disposal off and wandered back into the living room, sidestepping a box of books that she'd been meaning to unpack for...two years.

Two years since she'd beat feet from that crappy walk up studio in the West Village and she still wasn't fully unpacked.

She'd meant to get a bookshelf some weekend when she wasn't working. It just hadn't happened yet.

Her gaze travelled the room, taking in the stark white walls and the cardboard boxes tucked in the corner. It was nothing special. It wasn't even home. Not really.

It was just an apartment, a place to sleep and shower when she wasn't at the office.

It was also depressing as hell.

How had she let her life come to this?

She sighed. Her childhood on the pageant circuit had taught her that nothing in life came without some sort of string attached. And for her, the strings tended to tug on insecurities better left alone. It was so much easier to not connect in the first place.

Since she'd moved to the city, she'd done everything she could to push people away, never letting them get too close. She'd been so busy protecting herself and proving her worth she'd become cold and one-dimensional, like a paper doll.

Tears stung Olivia's eyes.

She blinked them back furiously, refusing to let them fall.

The last thing she needed to do was get herself all worked up and add a pounding headache to an already craptastic day. Besides, acknowledging them would mean that for the first time since she'd moved to New York, she had to admit she was lonely.

20

COLE

"MAN, is there anything Vixen hasn't tried in the last ten years?" Cole pushed pause on the sexy Vixen commercial blasting from his laptop.

"No," Olivia responded quietly, "and that's the problem. There hasn't been a lot of focus. McKenzie was all over the place, just throwing crap at the wall to see what stuck."

After subjecting himself to every commercial Vixen had ever run, he had to agree with her.

He shut off the media player. One more video and he'd reach sensory overload. Whether it was the strobe lights and techno music from the catwalk or the excess of bare skin, he wasn't sure.

Either way, he was a man who knew his limits.

And he'd reached them about five minutes ago.

"Agreed." He leaned back in his chair and clasped his fingers behind his head. "They've diluted the brand, which is an opportunity for us."

Olivia didn't respond. He wondered exactly what she was working on. She'd been uncharacteristically quiet the last half hour or so and her silence was killing him.

"You still with me?"

"Huh?" she responded, oblivious to his last question. He watched as she rubbed her thumb to her fingertips. First her right hand, then her left. Then both. "I'm sorry. What did you say?"

"I was just saying the Vixen brand has been diluted over the years," he remarked, studying her across the table. "That's an opportunity for us."

"Uh, yeah," she agreed, nodding slowly. She glanced briefly at the overhead light and rubbed her temple.

"Are you okay?" He knew better than to tell a woman she didn't look so good, but something was definitely off. "You seem...distracted?"

"I'm fine," she lied unconvincingly, her face twisting in pain.

When she placed a hand above her eyes to shield them from the light, he knew it was time to call it quits.

"Let's go," he ordered, closing his laptop and gathering the loose files from the table. "We're done for the night. It's getting late and we're both tired. We'll start fresh on Monday."

"Y—you go ahead," she said, resting her head against the back of the soft leather chair and closing her eyes. "I just need a minute to finish up here."

Bullshit. Sensitivity to light. Throbbing temples. He knew a migraine when he saw one.

He strode to the door and dimmed the lights. A tiny sigh of relief slipped from her lips, and his suspicions were confirmed.

"Do you get migraines often?"

"Yes. I mean, no." Olivia moaned, squeezing her eyes shut as tight as humanly possible. "It's none of your business."

He watched her struggling with the pain, feeling uncharacteristically hesitant for a moment before making his decision. He needed to help her, whether she liked it or not. She could barely open her eyes. There was no way she was getting home by herself.

Stubborn woman. How long had she felt it coming on and sat there working, too proud to call it an early night?

"What I meant to ask was, do you have anything to treat it?" he asked quietly. "A prescription, maybe?"

"It ran out," she murmured. "Haven't had time to pick it up."

Letting instinct take over, he pulled out his phone and dialed the hotel.

"Good evening. Thank you for calling—"

"Hello, James," he cut in before the concierge could finish reciting his standard spiel. He'd know the guy's voice anywhere. James was regularly offering his services and checking to see how his stay was going. Personal service seemed to be James's mission in life, not that he was complaining. "This is Cole Bennett. Listen, I need a favor. Can you have my car brought over to the office immediately?"

"Of course, Mr. Bennett. I'll make the call myself."

"Thank you. I'll meet the valet downstairs in five minutes." Cole disconnected the call and dropped the phone back in his pocket.

"What are you doing?" Olivia muttered.

"Taking care of you." He grabbed her laptop and stuffed it into her shoulder bag along with the tablet she'd been scribbling in. He scanned the room for any other personal belongings. "It's what friends do."

"We're not friends."

He gritted his teeth. They could revisit the topic of their friendship later when she was feeling better. Now certainly wasn't the time. She was getting paler by the minute.

"Fine. Then consider it protection of my investment. You're a valuable asset, but you're no good to me like this. Besides, there's no way in hell I'm letting you walk out that door alone when you can't even open your eyes."

"Don't worry—"

"Olivia," Cole started firmly, his mouth pressed into a grim line. "I am driving you home. Please do not argue with me about this. You can walk downstairs yourself or I can throw you over my shoulder and carry you. Your choice."

"I'll walk," she declared, giving him a defiant scowl.

He watched as she pulled herself to her feet using the edge of the table. She looked a little unsteady and weak in the knees. Maybe he should have just insisted on carrying her down to the car. It wasn't too late.

"Don't even think about it," she warned, as if reading his thoughts. He couldn't help but grin shamelessly. He'd need to work on his poker face. "Can you grab my coat and purse from my office? I'll meet you at the elevator."

He grabbed her things and they rode down to the lobby in silence. Cole ushered her past security with a nod of the head and out the front door to his waiting car. He tipped the valet and opened the passenger door open for Olivia.

"Nice ride," she mumbled as he tucked her into the passenger seat of his BMW coupe and fastened the seatbelt across her lap.

Cole jogged around the back of the car and slid into the driver's seat next to her, careful to shut his door as gently as possible to avoid causing her any additional discomfort.

"Where to?"

Olivia rattled off her address in Midtown as he pulled into traffic.

They rode in silence, with Cole stealing a sidelong glance at her every few minutes to see how she was holding up. He did his best to watch his speed and avoid jostling the car too much, but he could tell she wasn't tolerating the ride well. She didn't complain, but every now and then a little squeak would escape as he braked or hit a bump in the road.

When he pulled up in front of her building and double parked, her renewed protests fell on deaf ears.

"I can get upstairs by myself," she assured him, pulling her jacket tight around her shoulders to ward off the chilly spring breeze. "You're going to get a ticket."

"Trust me." He smiled and offered her his hand, which she took without argument. He looked up the block, taking note of the pharmacy two doors down, before shutting the door. "A parking ticket is the least of my concerns right now. Let's just get you up to bed."

Olivia led the way to her apartment, pausing at the door to dig the keys out of her purse. Her hand shook as she handed them to him. Fortunately, she didn't have a lot of keys on the ring, and he got it right on the second try.

He followed her into the dark apartment, thankful for the glow of city lights which provided just enough visibility to find the counter and drop her bags.

"Why don't you get changed and lie down?" he offered. "I'm going to run down to the pharmacy and see if I can get my hands on that prescription of yours."

She chewed on her bottom lip indecisively, but nodded. "Imitrex. It should be ready."

Fifteen minutes later he had secured street parking and made the pharmacy run, only to return and find Olivia sound asleep.

Not wanting to wake her, he grabbed a bottle of water from the fridge and set it on her nightstand with the prescription. It would be there if she woke during the night and needed it.

Her soft snores called to him, reminding him of their first night together.

A smile tugged at the corner of his mouth as he remembered how soundly she'd slept and how she'd burrowed under the covers. He indulged the memory by pulling her comforter up and tucking it around her shoulders. When a loose strand of hair fell on her cheek, he pushed it back without a second thought. Even asleep, she was beautiful, and for the first time, he sensed vulnerability in her tough exterior. He needed to comfort her, to reach out and stroke her hair, sweep his hands over her cheek, and take away her pain.

Seeing her there, so peaceful and serene with the moonlight casting a gentle glow across her face, he caught a flash of a different life. One that traded meaningless sex for evenings by the fire and the companionship of a woman whose happiness and well-being meant more to him than his own.

Only that life wasn't really meant for him. He'd learned that lesson well. Even if he wanted it, he'd just screw it up and it would fall apart.

Besides, it didn't really matter what he wanted. Olivia would never give him a chance. She'd made that abundantly clear.

21

———

OLIVIA

THE SMELL of fresh brewed coffee teased Olivia, testing her will to stay curled up in bed under the covers. She fought the good fight for about five waking seconds before abandoning the effort, her stomach leading the way to the kitchen. She shuffled down the short hall, finger-combing her hair and giving thanks to coffee fairies everywhere for the heavenly brew percolating in her coffee pot.

It was just what the doctor ordered after a skull splitting migraine.

She froze when she reached the kitchen and realized Rufus the fish had company. Sitting at her bar, looking irritatingly chipper as he worked on his iPad, was Cole.

What the hell was he doing in her kitchen? And why hadn't she taken the five seconds to brush her freaking hair? Or her teeth, for that matter?

"Good morning," he offered, giving her a dimpled grin and looking impossibly fresh.

Figures. Of course he'd be a morning person, something she could only claim after two cups of Espresso Roast.

"You're not the coffee fairy."

"I know nothing of coffee fairies," Cole admitted, grinning from ear to ear, "but I can offer you a piping cup and a hot breakfast. I figured you'd be hungry after last night."

"I'll be right back," she said, crossing her arms over her breasts self-consciously.

She was starving, but there was no way she was sitting down to breakfast with him wearing the world's thinnest, once-white tank top and no bra. She wasn't *that* hungry.

Olivia bolted back to her bedroom and threw a hoodie on over her tank. By the time she returned, Cole had laid out a smorgasbord of breakfast food. He had croissants, eggs, bacon, fruit salad, muffins, and yogurt. It was overkill, but her stomach growled appreciatively.

"I wasn't sure what you'd like," he explained, "so I got a little bit of everything. I might have gone overboard."

"Little bit," she joked, pinching her fingers together.

She didn't know what Cole was doing in her kitchen, but she wasn't about to let a hot meal go to waste when her cabinets were surely bare. She loaded up a plate and joined him at the bar.

"I didn't want to leave you alone until I was sure you were feeling okay," he offered as she bit into a buttery croissant. The flaky pastry melted on her tongue and she was sure she'd died and gone to heaven. She tore off a large chunk and popped it into her mouth. Simply. Divine. "You were in pretty rough shape last night," he reminded her.

The concern in his voice ripped Olivia from her food reverie.

Just as well. Probably best to clear the air before she ate herself into a food coma.

"I'm sorry about last night." She sighed, dropping the half-eaten croissant to her plate. Why had he come home with her anyway? She knew from personal experience he had better things to do on a Friday night than play Florence Nightingale. "I didn't mean to completely wreck your evening."

"You have nothing to apologize for." He reached out and touched her hand, sending a shiver racing down her spine. "I stayed because I wanted to. It's what friends do for each other."

"Yes, I seem to recall hearing that last night," she said, hastily removing her hand from his and tucking it safely between her knees. Now was not the time to let him get all touchy-feely, not when she still had warm fuzzies from him taking care of her the night before. "But, as you can see, I'm fine. Nothing a little sleep and a good meal can't fix. Speaking of which, thank you for breakfast."

"You're welcome." He eyed her seriously and Olivia fought the urge to wipe her mouth. Crap. Did she have jelly on her face? Hard to tell, but definitely possible. "I'm just glad to see you're feeling better."

"Good as new." She poked at her fruit salad. "In fact, once I get cleaned up, I'm going to head over to the office."

Cole bristled. She could actually see his body tense up at her words. "Why don't you relax and take the day off? There's no need to push yourself so hard."

"I'm fine. Besides, we only have two weeks left to pull something together for Vixen. Relaxation is a luxury we can't afford."

"You knew that migraine was coming on last night, didn't you?" he asked, leveling her with his eyes.

"What do you mean?" she countered, buying herself some time.

What did it matter if she knew? It couldn't be stopped.

And she really didn't want him to think the headaches were a regular occurrence. The last thing she needed was for him to decide she couldn't handle the pressure. She could handle the pressure as well as anyone.

"You kept rubbing your fingers together," he mused, "like you knew it was coming."

Damn him for being so freaking observant. She had two choices: lie and look like a weird, finger-rubbing freak or take her chances with the truth. As much as she hated showing weakness, the alternative didn't hold much appeal either.

"Sometimes I have an aura before a particularly bad migraine."

His face was a blank slate. "An aura?"

"It means I have early warning signs," she explained with a smile. Finally, something the man didn't know. "It's like pins and needles in my fingers, sort of like when your foot falls asleep."

"You are quite possibly the most stubborn human being on the face of the earth," he blurted out, shaking his head in disbelief. "Why didn't you say something? Your health is more important than any campaign."

"It's no big deal," she argued, crossing her arms and digging in her heels. "I figured we were almost done and they don't usually come on that fast."

"And you didn't want me to think you're weak and couldn't handle the pressure."

Damn, he was perceptive. "That, too," she admitted, avoiding his eyes.

"Olivia, no one in their right might would ever accuse you of being weak. We are going to nail that account. Together," he promised, an impish smile pulling at his lips as he studied her sweatshirt. "Right after you tell me what exactly an Apple Blossom Princess is?"

22

COLE

Olivia yawned and reached for her coffee. It was pushing midnight and they were the only ones left in the office. It had been like this for the last three days. Long hours, lots of frustration, and not nearly enough caffeine to balance it out.

Cole knew she was waiting for him to call it quits.

The woman was as stubborn as they came, which might have been sexy any other day. With the pressure mounting, they'd practically taken up residence in the conference room, abandoning their offices for the duration of the project. It was easier this way.

Easier except for the part where he was boxed up in a tiny, claustrophobic room, drowning in her scent and completely unable to concentrate on anything except all of the ways he wanted her.

It was counterproductive, to say the least.

He watched from beneath his lashes as Olivia stretched, arching her back. Such a simple gesture, but it unhinged him. The desire to caress her, run his hands over her body, rose unbidden. He'd been on his best behavior for the last couple of days, but it was getting old. He was tired of pretending he didn't want Olivia on her back screaming his name.

Even more so, he was tired of her denying their connection.

"You're kidding, right?" She threw his most recent proposal across the table. It skidded over the edge and landed in his lap.

"What's wrong with it?"

"Aside from the fact that it's tired?" Olivia scrunched her nose in disgust. "It's not even the right target audience."

"I beg to diff—"

"God, you are such a *man*." She rolled her eyes. "Always thinking with the *little* head. There's nothing new about supermodels strutting around in thong underwear, although I'm sure it's nice for you to look at."

Damn. Even her sarcasm was sexy. "I'd rather look at you."

Olivia stared directly at him. She wasn't smiling, but there was definitely a hint of...something...in her eyes for a moment before the cool mask came back down. "Has it occurred to you that *that* approach"—she nodded toward his proposal— "is exactly what got McKenzie fired?"

"Do you have a better idea?" he asked.

"Did you even look at the data?" she asked, as she began paging through the research binders she'd created. She highlighted something in yellow and passed the book to him. "Men only buy lingerie twice a year: anniversaries and Valentine's Day. Vixen needs a campaign that will draw regular, repeat customers. We need to make the *women* want it." She paused, then stared straight at him, challenging him to refute her assessment. "You're good at knowing what women want. Any ideas?"

He skimmed through the highlighted material. He was definitely distracted, but he couldn't argue with her logic. It was all right there in black and white.

Facts could be manipulated, but they didn't lie.

"This is really impressive, Olivia." He shouldn't have been surprised. He knew she was sharp, but he hadn't expected her to be such a talented researcher.

She managed to make even statistics sexy.

"Of course it is," Olivia said bluntly. "I know what I'm doing. I *was* on track to be partner a few weeks ago, remember?"

"Are you ever going to forgive me for that?"

"I don't have any current plans to, no." Olivia had turned her attention back to her binders.

Cole ran his fingers through his hair in frustration and let out a groan. "Do you have any idea how goddamn infuriating you can be?"

"*I'm* infuriating?" Olivia stood up from her chair and came toward him, her eyes blazing and her face flushed pink. "I'm not the one who keeps trying to fuck his *employee*."

God, she was so hot when she was angry.

He could smell her perfume from here, the scent of summer flooding his senses. His cock responded instantly. How the hell was he supposed to sit here, alone with her and surrounded by lingerie and pictures of half-naked women, and not think about bending her over the table and fucking the ever-loving daylights out of her?

She was smart and sexy, the kind of woman you couldn't let go of once you'd had a taste.

And he was only human, for fuck's sake, and they had unfinished business.

"Olivia." He looked directly at her. A deep flush swept down her neck and disappeared into the V of her blouse. The buttons strained against the soft cotton as her full breasts rose and fell with each shallow breath.

"Yeah?" She took a step toward him, not taking her eyes off his.

"I want to fuck you." He paused, letting his words hang in the air. "Right. Now."

Olivia's body reacted swiftly to the proclamation. Her nipples hardened. Her pupils dilated. "I want to fuck you, too," she said, almost too softly for him to hear, but her body was screaming signals he couldn't miss.

He needed to know if she was wet.

He stood, forcing the back of her legs against the table.

Olivia let out a low moan of pleasure. She looked up at him from beneath impossibly long lashes, lust churning in her eyes. Cole leaned into her, pressing his body to hers. She held her ground, strands of silky, honey-blonde hair tickling his cheek.

When he placed a hand on her stomach, she trembled and he could feel her muscles expand and contract at his touch, could feel her warmth through the thin fabric of her blouse. If he wasn't turned on already, that would have done the job. The way her body responded to him was empowering. His hand travelled up her stomach, splaying over her full breasts.

Cole paused. Olivia's heart hammered erratically against his palm, confirming her arousal.

He brushed his knuckles over her cheek, sweeping the loose hair back. He lowered his mouth to her ear, letting her feel the heat of his breath. "I want to bury myself so deep in you that you forget where you end and I begin."

"Yes."

It was a whisper, but it was all he needed.

Grabbing Olivia's hips, he lifted her onto the table. Her legs spread easily for him and he gave silent thanks for the loose-fitting skirt as he wedged himself between her soft thighs.

"Tonight, you're mine."

Olivia grabbed a fistful of his shirt, pulling him oh-so-temptingly close. She leaned in for a kiss, but he held her back.

Turnabout was fair play, and she'd been denying him for weeks.

"Not yet." He placed a hand on her chest, driving her down until her back was flat against the table. "I want to taste you first. *All* of you."

Olivia's hips twitched in anticipation as he pushed the silky fabric of her skirt up over her thighs, massaging and teasing along the way. His fingers slid over her hips, meeting no resistance, only milky white skin.

"No panties?" he growled, kneading the tender flesh between his fingers.

"Laundry day." She gave him a dirty smile. "Must be your lucky day."

Christ. He was hard as a rock. If he didn't get inside her soon, he wasn't going to last. But he always made good on his promises and he would have every inch of her before the night was through.

23

OLIVIA

This was happening.

Cole pulled her to the edge of the table and dropped to his knees. Things had escalated faster than she'd expected. She should put a stop to it. Like, right now.

Her heart leapt into her throat, a million emotions barreling toward her all at once.

With her head and body at war, she couldn't think straight.

His fingers massaged her thighs, easing a tension so deep she was certain it had settled into her bones.

When he placed a gentle kiss on her knee, lust won out.

She moaned as his tongue cut a path up the sensitive flesh of her inner thigh. The stubble lining his cheek pricked at the tender skin, creating a new and tantalizing sensation. She remembered the last time they'd come together and the ache between her legs grew, throbbing in anticipation. There was no turning back now. She was on dangerous ground letting him back in, she knew, but damn, he knew what he was doing.

Olivia surrendered to the moment, giving into the pleasure he offered here and now.

She melted in his hands as they slipped under her body, lifting her sex to him. She held her breath, desperate for contact.

When Cole's tongue darted out, tasting her, she cried out with pleasure, hips bucking toward heaven. He placed a firm hand on her abdomen, pinning her back to the cool table. He seemed to know her body better than she knew it herself as his tongue circled her, slipping between the folds of her skin and sending electricity shooting through her.

How was she supposed to give this up? No man had ever given her the kind of pleasure that Cole could provide. Whether it was experience or innate ability, she needed him.

With him, her inhibitions were stripped away, leaving only carnal pleasure the likes of which no other man could match.

"Christ, you're wet. You've been waiting for this all week, haven't you? Waiting for me to lick you right... *here*."

"Yes!" she cried out, desperate for more.

She needed his tongue, his fingers, his cock. She needed it all. With all of her nerves firing, she gripped the edge of the table as her body tensed for release. She called his name, begging him to push her over the edge into oblivion, but he refused to let her go. He was enjoying himself, maybe as much as she was, though she didn't know how that could even be possible.

Every time she neared climax, Cole pulled back.

Damn him. He enjoyed controlling her. She knew it all the way down to her curled toes.

He relished in the fact that he owned her body and could make it react to his every whim.

Olivia didn't think she could take much more as his tongue stroked the elusive cluster of nerves with a thousand dirty names. When his fingers plunged into her, keeping pace with his tongue, it was almost too much to bear. Her body arched off the table, rocking against him and seeking an outlet for the tension that had coiled deep inside of her. She exploded, ecstasy flooding her body as her muscles went limp, her feet dangling over the edge of the table.

Pushing herself up on an elbow, she watched as he climbed to his feet.

The hunger burning in his eyes called to her.

He was far from finished with her and she needed to give him something in return. After all, he wasn't the only one who knew how to give pleasure.

With steady hands, Olivia reached for his belt. She hooked her fingers in the waistband of his pants and jerked him close. "My turn."

Pressing her mouth to his, she ravished his lips. Their tongues battled for dominance, but in the end, she came out victorious. Cole would know the same pleasure he'd given her, but he also needed to know that she wouldn't always succumb to him.

Olivia wrestled with his belt, her kisses growing more savage as desperation set in. "Where the hell did you get this thing? Chastity Belts 'R' Us?"

Frustrated, she pinched his bottom lip between her teeth and held him there, releasing him only when his pants dropped to the floor and she was able to free his erection.

Stroking his length gently, she brushed her fingertips over the slick head.

"Fuck." He groaned. "That feels so good."

Cole wound his fingers through her hair, forcing her head back and exposing her neck to him. His mouth burned a trail of kisses down the curve of her throat and she struggled to remember that this was about him. If this was the last time they came together, she wanted to make sure it was memorable for both of them.

Olivia dropped from the table, standing face to face with him.

He wrapped his arms around her and she unbuttoned his shirt, running her hands over the chiseled muscles of his chest. He had beautiful skin, the kind most women would envy.

"You're perfect." She smiled. "But I guess you already knew that."

Cole laughed. "Flattery will get you everywhere, Sweetheart."

"Good to know," she replied, "because I have a destination in mind, just a little further south."

His hands moved up her back and into her hair, snapping the rubber band that held her ponytail. He tousled her hair, losing his fingers in the strands of silk as she fell to her knees. Wrapping her fingers firmly around his shaft, she sucked him between her swollen lips, taking him deep. She didn't know how much he could take, but she'd find out soon enough.

Olivia explored him with her tongue, teasing and stroking, finding dexterity she hadn't known she possessed.

He groaned for mercy she had no intention of giving.

Before she could finish, he brought Olivia to her feet and crushed her body to his, wrapping her tight in his embrace. He kissed her fiercely, reigniting the fire between her legs.

"Condom?"

"In my wallet."

She grabbed his pants from the floor and handed them to him.

He fished out the wallet and produced a foil square. He tore it open and unrolled it with experienced hands.

Determined to finish what she'd started, she threw him back on the table with a predatory smile. He stretched out, grinning appreciatively as she pulled up her skirt and climbed atop, straddling him.

His erection reached for her, begging for her touch.

Wrapping her hand around his thick shaft, she guided him to her center, lowering herself onto him in one delicious thrust. As their hips came together, she knew they wouldn't last long. She leaned back, enjoying the feel of his hardness sinking into her over and over. Riding him with a desperate rhythm, she ignored the pressure of the oak tabletop as her knees beat against it.

Sex with Cole had that effect.

Nothing else mattered when they were joined like this, wrapped in exquisite pleasure.

"I love the way your tits bounce when you're riding me. I could watch you all night."

And then his hands were under her skirt, massaging her inner thighs. She nearly lost her mind. His roving fingers made their way to the vee between her legs and when he rubbed his thumb across her clit, she moaned with pleasure.

A few more strokes and their bodies exploded in harmony.

Cole groaned, his release coming deep inside of her as her body clenched tightly around him, milking every last drop of pleasure from him.

When it was over, she collapsed on his chest, utterly spent.

They stayed like that for a while, catching their breath. She couldn't speak for Cole, but her mind was a blank slate in a state of post-coital bliss.

When she felt his lips on the top of her head, her heart skipped a beat.

Was that a kiss? A tender, gentle kiss?

Shit.

This was supposed to be about sex—*only sex*. Anything more than that was a string she couldn't—*wouldn't*—handle.

Her thoughts whirled in her head. *Pull it together, Olivia.* Cole didn't do romance. She was starting to see things that weren't there.

But he *had* stayed at her apartment all night to take care of her.

Insta-regret reared its ugly head and as quickly as it had come, her peace was shattered.

She pulled away from Cole and cast a weary glance at the table, which not ten minutes ago had her own bare ass on it. For god's sake, people would be eating lunch there tomorrow! How gross was that?

"It'll be fine," she reasoned, shaking her head.

The cleaning crew would come through and shine the damn thing with some Pledge or something, right?

"Olivia?"

Cole stood and stepped up behind her, placing a strong hand on her hip.

Her pulse quickened and she whirled on him, breaking the connection before she lost her nerve. He had a way of making her forget her resolve, as evidenced by their latest romp on the table.

"Look, this cannot happen again," she said, refusing to meet his eyes, afraid of what she'd see.

She already felt like a first-class bitch. Seeing it confirmed in those smoky gray eyes of his?

No thanks.

"What's the big deal?" he asked, tucking in his shirt and zipping his pants. He flashed her a devilish grin, the one with the dimples that made her weak in the already shaky knees. "Pritchard said, and I quote, 'I don't care what it takes'. We'll just tell him sex is part of the creative process."

"Cole, I'm serious."

"Who says I'm not?" he challenged, raising a brow and

adjusting his tie with practiced fingers. "We're good together. Why fight it?"

Olivia shook her head and sighed. "Look, maybe it doesn't matter for you. You're the boss. And a man. People would still take you seriously if you screwed every woman in this firm. But for me? It's trouble."

Cole had the audacity to laugh in response. "Sweetheart, as you keep reminding me, *I'm* your boss. Who exactly is going to get you in trouble for fucking me?"

He did kind of have a point. They were already working long hours together. Maybe adding in a few extra-curricular activities could be kept a secret.

It wasn't like they were planning a future together. They weren't even dating.

She chewed her bottom lip, mulling it over.

"Fine," she finally conceded, deciding to jump in feet first and do what she wanted for a change, even if it meant breaking the rules. After all, if anyone deserved to have a little fun, it was her. She grabbed her bag and started shoving files in it. "We're adults. We both like sex. Might as well hang on and enjoy the ride."

He looked skeptical. "But?"

For all his angling, it was clear he hadn't expected her to change her mind.

She was pretty damn surprised herself.

"But you *cannot* tell *anyone*. Sleeping with the boss is a credibility death sentence." She slung the weighty bag over her shoulder and turned toward the door. "I have a full schedule tomorrow. We'll pick up where we left off next week. We still have some time to come up with an angle for Vixen. We can't lose focus now."

24

COLE

THE SHARP TANG of disinfectant assaulted Cole's nose as he stepped through the sliding doors of the White Plains emergency room. The eye-watering, throat-burning stink reminded him just how much he disliked hospitals. He hated the look, the smell, and most of all the fact that someone close to him had been admitted for care.

As much as he loathed the place, he knew his little sister Anna hated it more.

That knowledge alone kept him moving forward when he wanted nothing more than to make a U-turn and cleanse his lungs with the fresh spring air outside.

Anna needed him and he had promised himself he'd always be there for her, no matter what.

He was determined to make good on that promise, even if it meant facing the ER and Olivia's wrath on the same day. He hated to miss the team meeting and the last thing he wanted to do was leave her hanging, especially now. They were finally on the same page with regard to sex and he didn't want to screw that up, but blood came before business.

Although their lives had taken different paths, he and Anna

had remained close over the years. While he had chosen a life of corporate bliss, Anna was the consummate suburbanite with a white picket fence and a pile of unruly children who, although he loved them dearly, regularly reaffirmed his bachelorhood.

Cole was nowhere near ready for kids.

He scanned the crowded waiting room.

It was a busy day and most of the cracked vinyl chairs were occupied with miserable looking souls seeking relief. Young, old, working class, and homeless, the emergency room was the great equalizer. There they all sat, ignoring the hum of daytime TV and waiting for the overworked doctors and nurses to call them back for treatment.

No Anna though.

Cole hoped her absence was a good sign.

He'd have been royally pissed if she was still waiting. Traffic had been horrendous and it had taken longer than expected to get to the hospital. The idea of his niece sitting there in pain all that time was unbearable.

He turned his attention to the harried looking receptionist, who was juggling two phones and typing simultaneously. He had to give the woman credit. She was the epitome of efficiency. He anxiously waited for her to hang up the phones, before approaching the desk.

"Hello," he started, giving her a dimpled smile. "My name is Cole Bennett and I'm looking for my niece, Lulu Kline. I believe she was admitted this morning."

The receptionist looked him over, the frazzled pinch of her lips softening as her gaze fell on his mouth. She batted her eyelashes and he had a pretty good idea what she was thinking.

"Broken arm, right?" she finally asked, typing on the keyboard. Her fingers flew over the keys, although her eyes remained fixed on him.

His stomach dropped. He'd hoped it was just a sprain or something.

Lulu was an accident-prone child, but she'd never broken anything before.

Unable to trust his voice, he nodded at the receptionist.

"We were expecting you," she explained, handing him a visitor's badge. "Let me just call someone to escort you back."

Cole followed an orderly who didn't look much older than Lulu through the labyrinth of exam rooms.

When they reached 113C, he knocked lightly on the door. The door swung open and Anna jumped to her feet. She sighed with relief when she saw Cole standing in the hall.

"It's about time," she said, giving him a half-smile.

Anna rushed forward to give him a hug.

Cole wrapped his arms around her tiny frame, which reminded him where Lulu got her frailness. Despite her feisty personality, Anna had always been delicate physically.

When she finally released him, he stepped back and studied his sister.

For all the traits they shared, dark hair, blue eyes and fair skin, there were just as many they didn't. Anna was petite, nearly a foot shorter, and had bone straight hair, unlike Cole, whose hair was out of control if not trimmed twice a month.

"I'm sorry," he apologized, squeezing her hand. "I got here as soon as I could. Traffic was a mess. You okay? Where's Joe?"

"He's at work," Anna explained. She pulled her hand from Cole's and sat on the bed next to Lulu, stroking her daughter's hair. Lulu gave him a shy smile. She looked more like her mother every day. Seeing her there in cutoff shorts with a dusting of freckles on her nose, reminded him of Anna at that age. "Joe couldn't get away. Besides, you know how he feels about hospitals."

Cole's temper flared.

Lulu had a broken arm and Anna hadn't been in a hospital in nearly two years, not since her miscarriage, and Joe couldn't take the fucking afternoon off? He knew that being in the hospital would tear open old wounds for Anna, which was another reason Joe should've been by her side, regardless of his own discomfort. He was her husband, for chrissake, and his family needed him.

What could be more important than that?

"Lulu, why don't you show Uncle Cole your cast?" Anna coaxed, changing the subject.

To his surprise, Lulu smiled and it lit up her whole face.

Cole took a deep breath and pushed his anger aside. He didn't want Lulu to see him angry. Joe was her father and he loved her, despite his many other shortcomings. After all, they were a family and that was a sacred bond, one Cole was unlikely to ever experience himself.

"Want to be the first to sign my cast, Uncle Cole?" Lulu asked, carefully holding up her plaster covered right arm.

She seemed to be in good spirits, which he attributed to the empty pill cup on the nightstand.

At least they'd given her something to manage the pain.

Cole was always impressed by the resilience of children, although it didn't increase his desire to start a family of his own any time soon. There was no place in his busy life for midday hysteria or afternoons in the ER.

"Lulu, how on earth did you break your arm?" he asked, shaking his head and eyeing her sternly. "You need to be more careful or you're going to give us all gray hair."

"It wasn't even my fault!" Lulu braced her good hand on her hip and cut her eyes at him. She was the spitting image of her mother. "It was Tommy's fault!"

"Was not either!" his nephew argued as he sauntered through the door with a can of orange soda in each hand. He put the drinks on the nightstand and rushed to Cole's side, flinging his arms around his midsection. "It wasn't my fault, Uncle Cole. We were just wrestling is all."

He ruffled Tommy's hair. "Maybe you better take it easy on your sister next time, what do you say?"

"Whatever! More like I better take it easy on him." Lulu chimed in. Tommy scrunched up his face and stuck his tongue out at his sister, but said nothing. "If I hadn't fallen off the-"

"There won't be a next time!" Anna corrected, giving both of her children a stern eye. "If I catch you wrestling in the house again, you'll both be grounded until you die."

She pretended not to notice when the kids rolled their eyes.

"So, where can I sign?" he asked, pointing to Lulu's cast.

He pulled a black pen from the breast pocket of his jacket. What the hell was he supposed to write on the cast of an eight-year-old girl, anyway?

"Anywhere you want, but don't write anything embarrassing!" Lulu giggled and offered her arm. He held it gently, afraid of pressing too hard and causing her discomfort. Placing the tip of the pen against her cast, he lightly scribed his name. "Can I be a flower girl in your wedding, Uncle Cole?"

He jerked his hand back as though she'd branded him with a flaming hot poker. "What makes you think I'm getting married?"

Anna snorted with laughter.

Lulu shrugged. "Well, mom said you had a new girlfriend, so I just thought..."

"Anna?" Cole eyed her curiously. "Care to explain what my niece is talking about?"

"What?" She crossed her arms and held Cole's stare. "I had to tell her something to get her mind off the pain. And I know there's someone new in your life, even if you insist on denying it. You're thinking about settling down. Why else would you have bought an apartment?"

"People buy homes all the time."

Anna smirked. "Yes, *people* do. But you're not *people*. You're Mr. I-never-stay-in-one-place-or-one-be—" She paused, searching for a more child friendly word. "*Relationship*-too-long."

Cole sighed heavily. Not only was Anna relentless, she had good instincts.

He couldn't get anything past her.

That also meant she didn't fall for his B.S. and lived by the sibling code, which she'd informed him on numerous occasions gave her the right to set him straight, even when her opinion left his oversized ego bruised and battered.

Hell, especially when it left his ego bruised and battered.

For some reason she was determined to teach him humility, although it hadn't exactly taken.

"It's about time you settled down. Who's the lucky woman?" she asked, grinning from ear to ear. "And when can I meet her?"

"First of all, there is no woman," he insisted, a little too forcefully, given he and Olivia weren't actually in a relationship and never would be. Not that he was opposed to the idea of Olivia at his new place. *That* he could actually picture easily. "Second of all, why would you even wish that on me?"

"Did you really just ask me why I would wish true love and happiness on my only brother?"

"Anna, you of all people should know I don't believe in that crap," he reminded her.

After all, hadn't they been raised by the same single mother when their deadbeat father walked out? If watching his mother break her back scrubbing floors to provide for them hadn't been enough to make him swear off marriage, Anna's own struggle to keep her marriage afloat would have surely sealed the deal.

There was no way he'd risk putting someone he cared about through all of that.

Hell, it was the reason he preferred to keep his relationships strictly physical.

An image of Olivia flashed in his head, and for the first time he wondered if he'd made a mistake. He respected the hell out of her and she deserved more than a quickie on the boardroom table. She deserved a man who could give her quiet nights making love by the fire, Sunday brunch, and someday, when she was ready, a family of her own.

Even if he wanted those things, he'd never be that guy. London had taught him that.

It had been an expensive lesson, costing him his company and his pride.

No, all he could offer Olivia was here and now.

"You know what your problem is, Cole?" He didn't know off hand, but he was pretty sure she was going to tell him whether he wanted to hear it or not. "You've never really been in love; the pulse pounding, butterflies in your stomach, cloud nine, can't eat, can't sleep, sacrificing your heart to someone you care about more than yourself, kind of love."

"As delightful as all that sounds, I'll pass, thanks."

"So there's no wedding?" Lulu asked, looking from her mother to Cole.

"Afraid not," he said, shaking his head and trying not to think too hard about all the things Olivia deserved that he couldn't give her.

"Bummer," she pouted, her bottom lip jutting out just like her mother's. "I was really hoping for a cool aunt!"

25

OLIVIA

Olivia adjusted her glasses irritably and sighed as she flopped gracelessly into her desk chair. With only two weeks left to create a mind-blowing pitch for Vixen, maybe her energy would be better used searching for a new job, because if today's strategy meeting was any indication, she was going to need it.

Cole hadn't even bothered to show up. And after he'd lectured her about being on time.

Where the hell was he anyway?

She glanced at the clock, confirming he was two hours late.

What could possibly be keeping him? It really wasn't like him to blow off meetings.

She hoped he was okay.

Wait. What? Since when did she worry about Cole's whereabouts? He was a grown man and perfectly capable of taking care of himself.

Besides, they weren't a couple. Just two people who liked to have sex. Together.

Nothing more, as evidenced by his no show today.

So much for partnering on this one. It was only the biggest account of her career, after all. No big deal.

Well, if that's how he wanted to play it, fine by her.

It would be a lot of work, but if she had to go it alone, that's what she'd do. She was no stranger to hard work, and she wasn't about to give up on her partnership or the Vixen account, not by a long shot.

Come hell or high water, she was going to land this account.

The question was, how?

Flipping through her notes, she jotted down follow ups and ideas that needed to be teased out for later. When Cole's massive body filled her door, she sensed his presence immediately.

"You're about two hours too late," she bit out, not bothering to look up. What was the point? He couldn't possibly have a decent excuse. Nothing short of a dead body—and he was very clearly breathing—would excuse his earlier absence. "And you had the nerve to lecture me on punctuality?"

"Didn't you get my message?" he asked, surprise coloring his words as he moved forward to claim the empty seat across from her.

Olivia sneaked a peek at him from under her lashes. She didn't know what he was talking about, but he looked about as sincere as a boy scout with those freaking dimples.

"What message?" she asked, exasperation creeping into her voice. Whether she was annoyed at him for being late or herself for noticing those dimples, she wasn't sure. "I've been in meetings all day. I only just got back to my desk."

"I'm guessing that one," he replied with a crooked smile as he pointed to the flashing red light on her desk phone. "I had an emergency and didn't want to leave you hanging with the impression I'd blown off the Vixen meeting."

"What kind of emergency?" she blurted out before she could stop herself.

If it was a real emergency, then it was none of her business.

She didn't want to know any more about him than she already did. Did she?

"The family kind," he explained. "I'm sorry, but it couldn't be helped."

Aside from the one call she'd interrupted with his sister, she'd never heard him talk about family before. When other people talked about their families or weekend plans, he usually remained quiet. He never talked about anything but business in the office.

Truth be told, she didn't know much about him at all. Curious, she flattened her brows, but remained silent.

"It's true." He blushed and rubbed the back of his neck. "I was in the emergency room with my niece. She broke her arm this morning wrestling with her brother."

"You were at the hospital?" Olivia asked, the skepticism on her face matching the tone of her words.

"I'm not a complete asshole, you know." He frowned, his gaze burning through her. She could practically see the wheels of his mind turning as he came to the realization that that was exactly what she thought. "My family needed me in White Plains. Otherwise, I would have been on time."

Her mouth fell open. "I'm sorry. I didn't...I hope she's okay."

"Kids will be kids, right?" he joked halfheartedly. "Lulu will be just fine. She's tough like her mom."

"Good," Olivia replied, cursing herself for exposing his softer side. That was the last thing she'd wanted to do. Getting to know him on more than a superficial level was too dangerous, given their chemistry. They had to keep things strictly business from now on.

Well, business with a splash of pleasure.

"So..." He rubbed his hands on his knees anxiously. "How was the meeting? What do you need me to do?"

"Glad you asked." She smiled, pleased that he was going to

let her take the lead for once without arguing. "I assigned the easy stuff, like fact-finding and consumer research, to the junior team members. Here's the breakdown of what everyone's working on. I've given them three days to deliver full reports to both of us."

"Looks like you've got everything covered," he said as he scanned the sheet she handed him. "And what will you and I be working on?"

"I'm glad you approve." She scribbled her address on a Post-it note, a very wicked idea forming in her mind. "I saved the hard part for us. Why don't you stop by my place tonight and we can work out the details?"

The look on Cole's face when she handed him the scrap of paper and winked at him? *Priceless.*

26

COLE

Cole didn't have to wait long after he knocked on Olivia's door. She answered wearing a sultry smile and a long t-shirt. No pants. It was the sexiest fucking thing he'd ever seen and apparently his cock agreed.

Olivia's lips twitched. "Took you long enough."

He growled in response and scooped her up in his arms. Down the hall, he found her room and laid her on the bed. He barely registered the details. They didn't matter. The only thing that mattered was getting inside his woman and proving once and for all that he alone could fulfil her needs so exquisitely.

When he stepped away from the bed, Olivia climbed to her knees and grabbed the waistband of his jeans.

"No games," she breathed, pulling him to her, their lips crashing together.

Her kiss was deep and desperate as he tore the clothes from her body, shedding them in record time before peeling off his own. His hands were everywhere all at once, exploring her soft curves as if for the first time. She was perfection. Perfect breasts, perfect ass, perfect legs.

And that little hollow in her neck? He'd never get tired of licking it.

Or the way she moaned when he nipped her with his teeth.

He thought he'd died and gone to heaven when she grabbed his cock, massaging the head with her thumb before reaching further south and cupping his balls. He groaned in agony as she stroked the sensitive flesh underneath. He needed to feel her body wrapped around him and he needed it bad. As they fell back on the bed together, he drove into her without warning.

Olivia cried out, giving him pause as she raked her manicured nails across his shoulder.

"Don't stop."

"You're sure?"

"Don't. Ever. Stop. Fucking. Me," she ordered, eyes ablaze.

"Wouldn't dream of it, sweetheart," he promised, twisting his hands in her hair and pulling out.

She whimpered at the temporary loss of contact as he flipped her over, intent on giving her such divine pleasure she'd be ruined for any other man. She complied easily, putting her hands against the headboard and lifting her bottom for him. He drove deep on the first stroke, burying himself to the hilt within her. She moaned and rocked her ass against him.

"Did you like that?"

"Yes!" she gasped, glancing over her shoulder at him with a coy smile.

He gave her bottom a firm slap and then rubbed it with the palm of his hand before sliding it up her spine and grasping her hair. He brought his mouth to her neck and dropped his other hand to her core, stroking the bundle of nerves that would make her beg for release.

His strokes came fast and furious as he buried himself in her, driving them both toward release as he angled for the spot that he knew would give her the best damn orgasm of her life. Their sweaty bodies rocked together as one. It was impossible to tell where one ended and the other began. They were connected on a level he had never known and damn if he wasn't enjoying every second of it.

"I want you to come for me right now," he ordered, rolling his thumb over the sensitive flesh between her legs.

"Yes!" she cried out as his final thrust drove them both over the brink into oblivion.

They collapsed on the bed, fully sated.

Olivia wriggled closer to him, closing the few small gaps the remained between their tangled bodies. He brushed her cheek and held her tight, cradling her head in his arm. With her body pressed to his, it was impossible to ignore the heat of her skin on his shoulder, the tickle of her hair on his face, or the beat of her heart on his chest. Lying there with swollen lips, flushed cheeks, and wrapped in only a sheet, she had never been more beautiful. And he had never been more satisfied.

Their little arrangement was working out perfectly.

Basking in the afterglow of great sex, Cole's gaze travelled the room, for the first time taking in the stark, functional space. There wasn't much to see, but the little black dress hanging from Olivia's closet door caught his attention. Definitely cocktail attire. Probably for the fundraiser Pritchard's wife was hosting.

If they were both going, maybe they should go together?

Show up, be seen, sneak out early, and have a little fun?

He dismissed the thought immediately. He had no business toying with such thoughts. It was too much like a date, and that kind of romantic nonsense was sure to screw up the good thing they had going.

With that in mind, he waited until she fell asleep, then slipped out of the bed, gathered his clothes, and headed for the door.

27

OLIVIA

OLIVIA PULLED the covers over her head, doing her best to ignore the sunlight streaming through her bedroom window. Why had she bought sheer curtains in the first place? Maybe if she didn't get out of bed, she could skip Saturday and fast-forward right to Sunday.

Unfortunately, her bladder had a different plan.

Sighing, she threw back the covers.

Cole was gone.

Good. No need for the messy morning-after business that had no place in their coworkers-with-benefits relationship.

She sat on the edge of her bed, glaring at the black cocktail dress that hung on the closet door, mocking her.

To say karma was a bitch wouldn't even begin to do justice to her current situation.

Pritchard's overly tan, overly plastic wife was having another lame fundraiser—save the platypus or something equally obscure—and she had no choice but to attend. It wasn't that she minded fundraisers. She was used to slogging through these things with a phony smile on her face and a check in her purse. The problem was that Chloe had snagged a date at the last minute, making Olivia the dreaded third wheel.

She had attended dozens of these things stag, and being alone didn't normally bother her, but what if Cole brought a date?

The prospect of showing up solo while he paraded around with another woman was a bitter pill to swallow.

Not that she was jealous.

He had every right to bring a date. They weren't together.

She slipped her feet into a pair of sock monkey slippers, and then shuffled into the bathroom. She was midway through brushing her teeth when her phone vibrated.

A picture of Chloe wearing a Cinco de Mayo sombrero flashed on the screen.

She wasn't done brushing her teeth, but she accepted the call anyway. Chloe wouldn't care.

"Whassup?" she asked through a mouth full of foam.

"Liv?" Chloe asked, sounding confused and no doubt wondering if she'd dialed the right number. "What are you doing?"

"Brushin my teef," she replied, wiping toothpaste from her chin with the back of her hand.

"Oh-kaay." Chloe giggled. "Actually, that's probably a good idea. Wouldn't want to show up for your date tonight with funky breath."

"Wha?" Olivia nearly choked. She spit out the toothpaste and wiped her mouth on a nearby towel. "What did you do, Chloe?"

"I think the words you're looking for are 'thank you'," her friend offered helpfully. "Anyway, I just did what you should have done all along. I called Alex. And it just so happens he's free tonight and would be more than happy to escort you to the Save the..." Olivia could easily picture Chloe racking her brain for the name of the ambiguous charity on the other end of the line, "whatever-it-is event."

"Chloe, what have I told you about setting me up?" Having weeknight drinks with Alex and pretending to be oblivious to Chloe's blatant matchmaking attempts was one thing, going on an actual Saturday night date with him was another.

"Funny thing about calling Alex," Chloe mused. "He was really surprised you'd want to go out tonight, you know, since you haven't returned any of his calls."

Olivia had resolutely *not* told Chloe about her most recent hookup with Cole, or their no-strings arrangement. It was also one of the reasons she was still dodging Alex's calls. How could she possibly go out with him when she'd been getting naked with another man?

"Chloe, you can't just go around making dates for me!" she complained, ignoring the thinly veiled question about Alex's unreturned phone calls.

"Why not?"

"Because it's rude!" Olivia sputtered. She rinsed her toothbrush and dropped it in the cup on the sink. "Besides, I was going to call him back. Eventually. I've just been really busy."

"Liar," Chloe challenged. "You haven't said two words about drinks with him. Did you really think you could avoid this discussion forever?"

"It's true. Cole's been making my life a living hell at work and I've been putting in a lot of extra hours," Olivia protested.

Maybe if Chloe was focused on something else, she wouldn't have to answer twenty questions about Alex. She still hadn't been able to decide if they should go on an actual date, which, apparently, was now the least of her problems.

"Oh, I have no doubt you've been pulling extra hours," Chloe agreed, "but don't tell me you can't find five minutes to call the poor guy back! He really likes you, Liv, despite the fact you've been blowing him off. If things with Cole are one and done, then why not give Alex a chance?"

"Look, Alex is a really nice guy, but I just don't have time right now."

"Make time!" Chloe argued. "Do you have any idea how long it took me to find Alex? Of course you don't," she rushed on, "because you never leave the office. Well, let me clue you in. It took *ages*. Nice, normal guys of the single, thirty-something, non-serial killer type are an endangered species, you know."

Olivia pressed her lips together.

She loved Chloe to death, but sometimes it seemed they were light years apart. If Chloe applied the same energy to her job as Junior Associate that she spent man hunting, she'd be stiff competition, but as it was, they had vastly different priorities in life.

"Seriously, Liv. Maybe Pritchard's wife could host a NYC man-raiser? Now that's a charity I could really get behind."

Olivia groaned and dragged a hand over her face.

"Remind me again why we're friends?"

"Because I have all the goods," Chloe chirped, sounding pleased she'd won yet another argument, "namely the Espresso Roast and the 411 on last-minute dates."

"Yes, that must be it," she relented, chewing on her lower lip. She needed a date and Alex was a nice guy. What was the big deal? It was just one date and it beat the hell out of showing up alone. "What time is Alex picking me up?"

28

COLE

COLE WAS MAKING THE ROUNDS, doing the obligatory schmoozing that was expected of him as a partner and a top donor. It was just after seven and he was already bored out of his mind. Until tonight, he'd never realized what a valuable asset a date was.

He hated these kinds of events, the kind where the sole purpose was to kiss ass and rub elbows. He didn't mind making worthy charitable donations, was happy to give them, but he could do without all the other bullshit. He just wanted to write a check and move on. He usually let his dates do all the socializing. They seemed to like it anyway.

Tonight was different, though. He grabbed a passing waiter and ordered a scotch.

Cole surveyed the garden as he waited for his drink.

It was a beautiful night for dancing under the stars. The sky was clear, there was a light spring breeze in the air, and the trees were aglow with sparkling white lights. The party was in full swing with a live quartet spilling classical music over the crowd. Donors drank and danced in harmony, although he would have bet most of them couldn't even remember the cause that united them this evening.

He hadn't seen Olivia yet, but he knew she was around somewhere. Probably in that sexy little black dress. Pritchard had intimated the event was mandatory, and she wasn't one to break the rules.

Well, most of the time.

The waiter returned with his scotch and he accepted it with a smile. He stood there sipping his drink, nodding at old acquaintances as they passed by. He didn't bother to engage in conversation. There was only one person he was interested in talking to.

Catching a glimpse of Olivia, he moved through the garden to intercept her.

Her hair was styled differently, falling in soft curls around her shoulders. It was an unusually feminine look for her, but if the hammering in his chest was any indication, it suited her perfectly. He immediately wished she'd wear her hair down more often so he could tangle his hands in those golden waves.

Cole weaved through the crowd, his eyes never leaving Olivia.

He still couldn't see her face, but he'd know those legs anywhere.

She was wearing the lacy black dress and fuck-me heels, a promise he hoped she'd deliver on later. His imagination teased him with images of Olivia strutting around his bedroom in those heels—those heels and nothing else.

As he got closer, he noticed Olivia was with a group. He recognized her friend Chloe from the office, but he'd never seen the men before. Olivia laughed at something the blond one said and rested her hand on his arm.

His blood ran cold. Who the hell was this guy, and why was she touching him?

They looked awfully friendly, and the significance wasn't lost on Cole. He had the sudden, inexplicable urge to punch a man he'd never even met.

Searching for a familiar face, he scanned the sea of bodies.

He smiled when Gabby appeared in front of him.

If anyone would know who Olivia was talking to, it would be Gabby. Pritchard's assistant had her finger on the gossip pulse of the whole agency.

"Evening, Gabby." Cole nodded his head politely. "This is some party, huh?"

"If you like this sort of thing." She smiled and took a sip of her wine. "Which I don't."

He laughed quietly. "I'll let you in on a little secret," he whispered. "I'm not a big fan either, but don't tell Pritchard."

"Your secret's safe with me," she promised.

Even in the low light, he could see she was blushing as a result of his attention. Gabby was rumored to be a gossip, but she seemed like a sweet girl, albeit one who was in way over her head at the office.

Cole glanced around casually. "Do you know who Olivia's talking to? I don't think I've met him yet," he said, playing dumb. "I can't recall seeing him around the office."

"Oh, you wouldn't have," Gabby confirmed, happy to share her knowledge with the boss. "He doesn't work at PBA. He's Olivia's date. Must be serious too, because she's *never* brought a date to one of these things."

A muscle in Cole's jaw ticked as he ground his teeth together.

She'd brought a date? Just a few days ago he was on his knees devouring her and here she was with a date? Flaunting it in his face?

"I guess there's a first time for everything." Gabby laughed. "Who knows? Maybe Olivia will finally get laid and loosen up a little."

Cole leveled her with his eyes. "Excuse me."

Then he turned and stalked toward Olivia, an emotion he couldn't name twisting in his gut.

29

OLIVIA

OLIVIA FELT a familiar tingle low in her belly as her inner sex kitten roared to life.

Cole.

She'd hoped to avoid him this evening, keeping Alex at the edge of the crowd, but it seemed her luck had just run out. He was headed right toward them and closing in fast, the look on his face anything but friendly.

She summoned the most sincere smile she could and hoped for the best as Cole reached the edge of their little group.

"Cole, it's so nice to see you."

"Olivia, Chloe." Cole nodded formally, his gaze settling on Alex. The hard set of his jaw was a stark contrast to the soft glow of the garden lights reflected in his silver eyes. He wore a black tux that Olivia was sure must have been tailor made. The cut of the jacket emphasized his broad shoulders and trim waist, doing little to distract her from the rock-hard abs she knew lay beneath. The man had good genes, and the damn thing fit like a glove. "Lovely as always. And who are these lucky bastards?"

Olivia prayed for lightning, a black hole, or even a good old fashioned fainting spell—anything to escape. Chloe on the other hand, relished the opportunity to introduce their dates, completely oblivious to Olivia's growing horror and the dangerous edge to Cole's anything-but-innocent question.

"They are lucky, aren't they?" Chloe gushed, waving her glass. "This is Kyle." She poked her date in the ribs with her free hand. "And that Ken doll over there is Alex."

Olivia searched the heavens. This had to be a friggin' cosmic joke.

Chloe needed to be cut off—*STAT*. And, really, didn't she have enough problems already without adding a tipsy BFF to the mix? Before she could come up with anything intelligent to redirect the conversation, Chloe babbled on.

"Aren't they adorable?" Chloe flashed Cole a thousand-watt smile, daring him to disagree. "Just like a real live Barbie and Ken, right?"

Olivia's cheeks flamed. She was going to kill Chloe.

To his credit, Alex rolled with the introduction as if being compared to a plastic, sexless doll was an everyday occurrence. He extended his hand to Cole with as much dignity as possible and gave a firm shake.

"Alex, this is Cole Bennett," she explained, "my boss."

"Nice to meet you."

God, Alex was a good sport. She mentally gave him bonus points for that alone.

"Likewise," Cole agreed. His tone was friendly, but his eyes were ice as he addressed Alex. "And what do you do, Alex? I know you're not in advertising, because I don't recognize you."

"Oh, do you know everyone in the business?" Alex asked, ignoring Cole's blatant dig.

"Job hazard, I'm afraid." Cole shrugged, ratcheting the tension up a few more notches. "When you own a company as big as PBA, it pays to keep an eye on all the little guys."

"I'm sure it does." Alex bristled. Olivia didn't blame him. She was thinking about kicking Cole in the shin herself just to put an end to the pissing match. "I actually work on Wall Street," Alex explained.

Olivia took a gulp of her wine. If ever someone were going to drop a house on her, now would be the time.

"Really?" Cole asked, clapping Alex on the back. "I didn't think there was much money in stocks these days. Last I heard the country was in a recession."

"I do all right," Alex replied, shrugging off Cole's hand. His mouth was smiling, but his eyes were hard. It didn't take a genius to figure out what was going on. Olivia prayed for rain, lots and lots of rain. "But truth be told, I tend to focus on the important things in life, like enjoying the company of this beautiful woman right here."

Just when she thought things couldn't possibly get any worse, Alex slipped his arm around her waist, pulling her close and boldly staking his claim.

"Some guys just have all the luck," Chloe explained, goading Cole with a smirk. Thankfully, Kyle took the opportunity to grab her empty wineglass. He looked like he'd rather be anywhere else. Olivia couldn't blame him. She was debating the merits of a cut and run herself. Maybe they could share a cab. "Lucky in life *and* lucky in love," Chloe giggled in a sing-song voice.

"So it would seem. It is nice to see Olivia getting out and having a little fun for a change." Cole smirked, looking her over from head to toe. Heat tore through Olivia, her hammering heart pumping molten lava through her veins as if Cole had touched her physically. "You are having fun, aren't you Olivia?"

"Of course," Olivia returned through clenched teeth. She wasn't big into daydreams, but even if she'd harbored fantasies about two men fighting over her, it wouldn't have been like this! She gave Cole an insincere smile. "It's such a wonderful cause. But we've taken up enough of your time this evening, Cole. We don't want to keep you from the other guests. After all, who are we to deprive all these lovely ladies of your company?"

She turned her back to him and steered Alex toward the nearest waiter holding champagne.

Ignoring etiquette entirely, she grabbed two and downed them both, replacing the empty glasses on the tray. To his credit, the waiter seemed completely unfazed. She guessed there was probably a lot of someone-I-stupidly-slept-with-on-a-dare-just-completely-embarrassed-me-in-public drinking at these things.

The champagne warmed her from the inside out, and she began to relax a little.

Until she felt a tap on her shoulder.

She turned to see Lexie, a Junior Associate on her team, beaming at her. "Olivia! I thought it was you! You look soooo pretty." Her words were slurring a little bit. "Oh my gosh, who's the cutie you're with?" She ran her eyes up and down Alex with a connoisseur's glance.

Olivia smiled wearily. "Lexie, Alex. He works on Wall Street. Alex, Lexie. She's a Junior Associate at my agency."

Lexie giggled. She had clearly been hitting the free champagne hard. "I'm totally surprised you're not here with Cole," she stage-whispered, winking conspiratorially at Olivia. "Everyone at the office was betting you were a thing." She glanced at Alex. "Oops, sorry."

Olivia shot Lexie a killer glare. "No," she said vehemently. "My *boss* Cole Bennett and I are *not* a thing. We have never been a thing. We will never be a thing."

She realized too late that Cole was standing right behind her.

30

OLIVIA

Olivia excused herself under the pretense of finding the ladies' room and made a beeline for the house. She didn't actually need to use the bathroom, but Cole had ducked inside not five minutes earlier and she had every intention of hunting him down. What she was going to do when she found him, she had no idea.

Suffice it to say, he was going to get a very explicit piece of her mind and she didn't care who heard. In fact, the more the merrier. A public ass chewing would do wonders for his overinflated ego.

Hell, it was a wonder his head fit through the damn door in the first place.

He'd been a complete jerk to Alex, throwing his money around and acting like a total prick. And for what? What was his problem anyway? He had a crap-ton of money, an infinite supply of gorgeous women, and Olivia's dream job.

What more did he want? Couldn't he just butt out of her life already?

Olivia stalked up the stone steps and twisted the knob on the front door. She pushed the shiny, black monstrosity wide open and let herself into the grand foyer without hesitating.

A blast of frigid air met her at the door, raising goose bumps on her forearms. The pungent scent of fresh cut flowers wafted through the open space, rolling off the largest arrangement of purple orchids she had ever seen. Above, an antique crystal chandelier hung from the ceiling, casting twinkling lights across the marble floor. A wide, curving staircase opened in front of her with narrow halls branching off to the left and right.

The place felt more like a hotel lobby than a residence. The only thing missing was an English butler.

Old money at its finest. She wrinkled her nose in distaste.

There was no way she'd ever live in a place like this.

Looking around, she decided to try the hall on the right. He couldn't have gone far and the sound of bustling caterers carried from the back of the house. Besides, she hoped it would be warmer in the kitchen with the ovens running.

Making her way down the hall, she rubbed her arms to chase away the chill.

She squeezed past a slight girl with a tray full of hors d'oeuvres that smelled heavenly. Her stomach grumbled in protest, but she forged on without a backward glance.

She was a woman on a mission.

Olivia crept into the kitchen, doing her best to stay out of the way.

The room was in chaos with shouted orders, banging pans, and the roar of the gas stovetop. If she had any interest in the culinary arts, she might've envied the kitchen, but as it was, she could barely scramble an egg, so the expansive kitchen was nothing more than an irritation as she moved among the warming trays that had been jammed into every open corner. She skirted the sous chef and muttered in frustration.

Where the hell was Cole?

"Looking for someone?"

Olivia whipped around to find him standing behind her, leaning on an unmarked door and looking irritatingly sexy.

"As a matter of fact—" she started. Before she could finish, he grabbed her wrist and pulled her through the door, which turned out to be a dimly lit pantry the size of her apartment.

The pantry walls were lined floor to ceiling with shelves, and there were three little aisles created by additional rows of shelving, all of which were fully stocked. These people did a hell of a lot of entertaining or they were preparing for the apocalypse. There was enough food stashed away to feed a third world country.

What a waste.

Cole shut the door, sealing them inside the dank stone pantry. The door clicked shut with a resounding echo and all thoughts of world hunger dropped from her consciousness.

"What the hell is wrong with you?" she asked, planting a hand on her hip and taking the offensive.

He was *not* getting off the hook this time.

"What the hell is wrong with me?" He smirked, his brows knit together in disbelief. He took a step forward and Olivia's heart fluttered. She was determined to hold her ground, although the urge to retreat was growing—*fast*. The pantry might be ridiculously large, but it wasn't big enough for the two of them. She shouldn't be this close to Cole, not alone, not even when she was pissed beyond belief. It was too dangerous, since she had yet to find a cure for I-hate-you-but-I-want-to-fuck-your-brains-out-itis. "You're kidding, right?"

"Do I look like I'm kidding?" she asked, fighting to control her anger and hoping the noise of the kitchen would mask their words.

She was having second thoughts about the whole 'the more the merrier' notion. The last thing she needed was a rumor about another knockdown-drag-out with Cole getting around the office. She'd been the subject of enough office gossip to last a lifetime, thank you very much.

"Hey, I'm not the one who brought the douchebag." Cole cocked his hip and leaned into one of the metal racks looking self-satisfied at his little joke.

He was being a complete ass, but damned if he didn't look good with those dark waves spilling over his forehead. He studied her, his eyes churning with anger, or maybe amusement?

Olivia couldn't identify the emotion, just as she couldn't be sure if it was lust or rage causing her own heart to beat spastically in her chest. She told herself it was anger. It had to be. Her traitorous heart definitely wasn't thinking about all of the delicious things he could do with that mouth of his.

That would just be wrong.

"The only douchebag out there was you," she spat, digging her nails into the palms of her hands. "What do you care anyway? You're not my boyfriend. In case you forgot, the only thing going on between you and me is crazy monkey sex."

Cole pushed off the rack.

He was on her in a flash, trapping her between his powerful arms, his hands braced against the shelves behind her.

"You made that *perfectly* clear out there," he growled. His gray eyes were smoldering under his lashes. Her pulse skyrocketed. "We're *definitely* not a thing, right?"

"You don't get to have it both ways," Olivia said, raising her chin defiantly. "You don't get to say we'll just have sex, no strings attached, no emotional involvement, and then be a total possessive jackass to the only date I've had in years."

Cole shot her a dark look and snorted. "Who, Wall Street? You can do better than that, Olivia."

"Did you even hear what people were saying? I told you not

to tell anyone. I told you they'd find out. I told you…" Olivia trailed off, unable to finish due to the sudden rock in her throat.

Cole shook his head. He dropped his arms and she could breathe again. Then he stepped away, turning his back to her as he walked the length of the pantry.

She couldn't read his mind, but his body language spoke volumes as he laced his fingers behind his head. He was clearly struggling. With what exactly, she didn't know.

"Look, I'm sorry," Cole said. "But it doesn't matter what they think."

"Doesn't matter to who?" Olivia snapped. "Because it sure as hell *matters* to me. I don't know how you ended up so fancy that you could just swoop in and steal my partnership and have nothing matter to you, but I worked my way to where I am. I have fought for years against jerks who said I was just a pretty face and a hot ass that slept her way up the corporate ladder." Olivia paused to take a deep breath, her heart hammering against her ribcage. "And now, thanks to you, everyone is, once again, saying I've fucked my way to the top."

"I can tell them—"

"*No*," Olivia said emphatically. "You've said more than enough. I don't need you to defend my reputation. I need you to get the hell out of my head."

"This thing between us, it's not going away. I'm not going away." He closed the distance between them, leaving only inches between their bodies. Tension crackled in the air, an undeniable reminder of their explosive chemistry. "We're so good together, Olivia. We shouldn't let a bunch of ignorant gossips screw it up." He stroked her cheek, his eyes fixed on hers. His breath came hard and fast. She wondered if his blood pressure was as close to the danger zone as her own. "Tell me what you want, and I'll do it."

"I don't know," she whispered.

What *did* she want?

She'd been so convinced that their sex was just meaningless fun to him that his reaction to seeing her with Alex had caught her off guard. Was it possible he wanted more? He hadn't actually said he felt anything more for her than unbridled lust—which, she had to admit, was still worth a hell of a lot—but the way he'd acted so...hurt when she'd insisted to Lexie they weren't dating.

And then there was the way he'd completely insulted Alex.

Was she just seeing what she wanted to see, or was there more?

It had been so long since she had opened herself up to a man, she'd be crazy to start with this one. If she let him in and he broke her heart, she'd never be able to put those pieces back together again. She knew beyond a shadow of a doubt this man had the potential to obliterate her.

It was impossible to think with him crowding her.

She turned her head, refusing to look him in the eye. It didn't help. With his breath scorching her cheek, rational thought slipped through her fingers like sand through an hourglass.

"I can make you forget about Wall Street," he swore, the intensity of his words sending a shiver down her spine and melting her resolve.

Cole dropped his mouth to her collarbone, placing a tender kiss on her bare skin and she knew she was a goner. How could she resist him when his soft lips were pressed to the delicate flesh of her neck like that?

His mouth lingered and she basked in the intimacy of the act and the unsought-for connection that seemed to have a will of its own, growing stronger each day. He brought his tongue up along the side of her neck, kissing, tasting, tempting, as he pressed his erection to her belly.

Olivia wriggled against his hardness. She was burning up, heat coursing through her body as it begged for more.

Running his hands over her hips, he gripped her ass and pulled her closer. When his knee slipped between her thighs, she knew she should tell him to stop. She was with Alex tonight. Sure, they didn't have a commitment of any kind, but that didn't mean it was okay to make out with Cole in a closet.

Or did it?

How could anything that felt so good be wrong? It couldn't be. She was sure of it.

Besides, the look in Cole's eyes was bordering on orgasmic. He wanted her and he wanted her *now*. And you know what? Her vagina sort of wanted him too.

Just one more time. What could it hurt?

She ground her hips against him, enjoying the friction of his thigh between her legs as he inched her dress up revealing a red lace thong. He pulled back, pinning her to the rack as his eyes raked over her half-naked body. When they flitted from her bare legs to the pantry door, it was obvious what he was thinking: *no lock*.

With a growl, Cole pulled her into his arms and swept her deeper into the pantry.

"I'm not taking any chances," he purred. "The way you look in that dress? I'm keeping you all to myself."

Safely between the shelves and in the darkest corner of the room, he resumed his exploration of her body which had abandoned all pretense of resistance. His hand skimmed across her abdomen, snaking down the front of her panties. When he ran his thumb over her wet heat, she forgot all about the stone wall jutting into her back. She forgot about the party, the caterers, and the fact they were getting it on in a glorified closet.

Olivia moaned, arching her back as his thumb swept a wide,

teasing circle between her legs. She cursed the scrap of damp satin keeping his fingers from her body.

If only it were laundry day.

Cole's eyes bore into her as he pushed her panties aside. She held her breath, silently willing him to claim her.

God, he was intense. In the office Olivia was always in control, but with him she felt reckless and wild. He owned her body and there was nothing she could do but relax and enjoy the ride.

Well, *almost* nothing.

The urge to feel Cole's mouth on her struck, bringing with it a desperate need to join her body with his. Olivia leaned forward at the exact moment he slipped his fingers into her. She cried out, the sounds of her pleasure muffled by his lips moving hungrily over hers. Electricity exploded through Olivia's body, her muscles tightening in anticipation as his fingers moved in and out of her.

The pace was slow at first, quickly accelerating to a frenzy, his thumb circling the sensitive nerves that would push her to climax. She threw her head back and relaxed into him, letting him support her weight while her conscience chastised her for giving into her carnal urges.

Again.

What was wrong with her? Why couldn't she tell this man no?

Probably because he had the most amazing hands on the planet.

Her body tensed up, preparing for the explosive finale that Cole's touch promised to bring.

"We shouldn't be doing this," she panted. "Alex..."

"Fuck Wall Street." Cole rolled his thumb over her clit and she saw stars. Her body shattered in orgasm, bucking against the warmth of his hand. "You belong with a real man, Olivia. You belong with me."

"I can't," she whispered. "Sleeping with the boss in secret is one thing, but openly? No one would ever take me seriously again. I've worked too hard—"

"You've proven yourself a hundred times over at PBA!" he argued. "Anyone with half a brain can see that. Hell, Jonathan should have promoted you ages ago. You have to stop worrying so much about what other people think or you'll make yourself crazy."

Olivia sighed. "You don't get it. It's not just about what other people think. It's about me earning my place—and my promotion—on my own merit."

He growled, the sound deep and low, filled with frustration. He pulled away, giving her some much-needed but somehow unwanted space, and thrust his hands into his pockets.

"Fine. I know what I want. And what I want is to fuck you, whenever I want to, without giving a damn about what some fucking teenage assistant says about it." He reached for the doorknob. "Let me know when you figure out whatever the hell it is *you* want."

31

OLIVIA

"Please see that Cole gets these immediately." Olivia handed Jack a stack of folders with her latest ideas and storyboards.

"I'll run them over—"

"That won't be necessary," Cole interrupted, as he barged in. He grabbed the files from Jack, towering over the kid and standing a little too close. "Thanks, Jack. Appreciate your help. I can take it from here."

Jack looked at Olivia uncertainly before he scampered away.

"You shouldn't do that to him," she chided.

"I don't know what you're talking about," he countered, a smile pulling at the corners of his mouth.

As if he didn't know what she meant. He clearly got a kick out of messing with Jack's head, leaving her the daunting task of building the kid's confidence back up, day in and day out. She frowned at him, but held her tongue. Arguing wasn't going to get her anywhere and they had much bigger problems than Jack.

"You can't avoid me forever, you know." Cole stripped off his jacket and tossed it on the back of an empty chair, narrowing the distance between them. He crossed his arms, flexing the muscles of his rock-hard biceps.

A burning need to touch him stirred deep within her.

She remembered the feel of those arms wrapped around her last weekend and she longed to get it back. But he was right. They needed to get off this lust/hate rollercoaster.

It wasn't good for either one of them.

Easier said than done.

If only the man wasn't so freaking hot. Couldn't he just be like the other frumpy slobs running around the office? Then she'd have no trouble ignoring him.

"Don't be so sure about that," she responded, doing her best to wrestle her undersexed libido into submission.

She'd been avoiding him as much as possible for the last couple of days, using Jack and other Junior Associates to run interference. She knew he'd come around eventually, but she hadn't expected it to happen so fast.

"We need to hammer things out for the Vixen pitch. We're running out of time."

She sighed. He had a point. The clock was ticking and both their reputations were on the line.

Cole sat on the edge of the table, crowding her as he'd done Jack.

She ignored him, fiddling with her glasses. Why was she wearing them anyway? It wasn't like she needed them; they were really only good for reading small print. It was more habit, she supposed. She had noticed a long time ago the more intellectual she looked, the more weight her ideas carried.

She threw the stupid glasses on the table.

Cole raised a curious eyebrow, but said nothing.

"What did you have in mind?"

Something wicked flared in his eyes as they bored into her with an intensity she'd never seen before. Her heart clenched and for a moment she feared he could see her every thought, her every desire. Really, how did he expect her to concentrate when he was looking at her like that, like he might devour her any second?

"Down, boy." She thrust out her chin. Sure, it was impossible to form a coherent thought with his bits so close to her face, but she wouldn't let him turn her into a puddle of goo. They had work to do. "Can you turn it back a notch already?"

To her surprise, he threw his head back and laughed. It was a beautiful sound, the kind most women dreamed of coming home to at night. But Olivia wasn't most women.

Cole pushed off the table and rose to his feet.

She sighed with relief when he moved to the window, giving her some breathing room. She watched as he rolled up his sleeves, revealing well-muscled forearms. Blood went rushing to her core, riding on a wave of arousal.

So much for breathing room.

"Think," he urged, locking his fingers behind his head. "This shouldn't be so hard. You're the target audience, right? A modern woman, hear you roar and all that?"

"If you'd asked me a month ago, I'd have said yes. Now?" She grinned. "Not so much. In case you haven't noticed, I'm still paying the price for my last hurrah." Olivia shrugged. "Bad karma, I guess."

He glowered at her. "Can you be serious for a minute?"

Jeez. Since when did Cole turn into Mr. Seriouspants? She rolled her shoulders, shaking off her sarcasm, and put on her game face. "What's your point?"

"What do women want?"

"I don't know." She drummed her fingers on the tabletop as she thought about it. What did she want? "To be taken seriously? Treated like equals?"

"I'd feel better about that response if it didn't sound like a question."

Olivia stretched and slipped out of her jacket. The first heat wave of summer had arrived early, turning the conference room into a freaking sauna, and the A/C was struggling to keep up.

Then again, maybe it wasn't the temperature so much as the memory of Cole feasting on her in this very room—on this very table—that had her body simmering. What the hell had she been thinking anyway?

His intense gaze burned through her, ripping her from her thoughts. His eyes radiated sex as he stared at her bare arm with lust. Olivia glanced down, realizing too late the strap of her red lace bra had slipped loose. She hastily pushed it back up, hiding it under the sleeveless cami. This wasn't the time to get carried away by their hormones. They needed a campaign strategy, and they needed it now.

32

COLE

COLE DIDN'T CONSIDER himself a genius by any stretch of the imagination, but every now and then he had his moments. As he watched Olivia tuck the strap of her hard-on-inducing bra back in her shirt, inspiration struck. And it was an honest to goddamn epiphany.

It was so obvious.

The Vixen angle had been right in front of them all along, but they were too busy fighting to see it.

"I've got it," he announced. He pulled a chair up to the table and sat across from Olivia. "I know what women want."

"Really? You know what women want? Outside of the bedroom?" She wrinkled her nose. "Because I don't really think Vixen is looking for a how-to tutorial on pleasing your one-night stand."

He shot her a dark look, but let it slide. "Look at you. You make a point of downplaying your assets so you aren't accused of trading on looks, right?"

She chewed on her bottom lip. "Yeah, well, between the boys club and the kitty claws, I have to work twice as hard for respect."

For the first time, he felt like she was sharing something real, a piece of herself she'd kept hidden far too long. It felt surprisingly good and he wanted more.

"I'll bet a lot of women feel like you do, and yet, there isn't a single lingerie company in the market that recognizes real, working women. Lingerie ads focus on supermodels and soccer moms."

"Tell me about it." She rolled her eyes. "It's like sexy on steroids—which real women can't live up to—or granny panties —which doesn't exactly inspire lights-on-for-sex confidence."

"Exactly. There's no middle ground," he agreed, thrilled she was buying into the idea. It was the right approach. He could feel it in his bones, but he needed her onboard and fully committed to make it work. They couldn't afford to be split on this one. "Where does that leave a young working woman like you who aspires to more?"

Doubt lined her eyes. She flattened her brows and he knew he was losing her. She was a textbook example, but he couldn't make it too personal or she'd balk at the whole thing.

"Where are you going with this?"

"Smart. Confident. Sexy as hell. That's our audience," he explained as he moved around the table, coming to rest behind her. He leaned down, bringing his mouth to her ear. "From the boardroom to the bedroom... Be a Vixen."

Her sharp intake of breath told him he'd nailed it. It also put him in mind of her aroused face, but he did his best to push that thought aside. She'd made it clear at the fundraiser that she was done with their little arrangement, which was probably for the best anyway. Rules were rules, and he was beginning to be uncomfortable with how often he found himself thinking about Olivia.

"I like it," she announced, once again all business. And damn if he didn't find that arousing. He lo—no, *appreciated*, her take-charge sassiness, even when she was dishing it his way. "We've got a tagline. What else have you got?"

"We emphasize sharp women in powerful positions. It'll have to be sexy, but believable."

"It's risky," she pointed out. "If we screw it up, we'll just alienate people. The women have to be authentic and so does the motivation. If the idea is to empower women, then we have to sell it right."

"I'm more worried about competing effectively with prime-time fashion shows without supermodels of our own."

Olivia groaned. "It's a wonder you survive yourself. Do you ever think about anything but sex? Seriously?" she asked, shaking her head.

Cole gave her a cocky grin and shrugged. "Might as well focus on the things I'm good at."

"Do you really think women like me sit around and watch anorexic supermodels strut around on the catwalk?" With her hand on her hip, she reminded him of his sister, the other spitfire in his life with attitude to spare. "Or do you think it's more likely men like you watch that crap? Men, need I remind you, who don't actually buy lingerie anyway. Check the research."

She tossed one of her binders at him.

He caught it easily and pushed it to the side.

"I don't need to look at the data." He combed a hand through his hair. She must really think he was a sex-crazed idiot. He wanted to point out the 'Be a Vixen' angle was his idea in the first place, and he wasn't a moron. He certainly didn't become a partner at PBA by being a completely useless jackass, but then again, why would she think any differently? He was constantly trying to get under her skirt. Not to mention the fact they hadn't managed to come up with anything constructive or usable in the last few weeks. Hell of a way to start his new job. "I remember.

Men's lingerie purchases are minimal and seasonally driven. We need to attract loyal, repeat customers," he recited dutifully, raising his palms in a gesture of surrender.

"Good. I'm glad to see you were paying attention." She gave him a curt nod and replaced her glasses. "Just keep in mind this has to be subtle. We'll need a robust digital campaign, something that will go viral."

Cole laughed and shook his head in disbelief.

He wasn't sure how it had happened, but suddenly he was taking orders from her?

Then again, he kind of liked it. She knew what she was doing in the boardroom *and* the bedroom. She deserved to take the reins on the Vixen account.

Hell, she deserved to be partner.

33

OLIVIA

EXHAUSTED, Olivia crossed her arms on the desk blotter and buried her face. The hours they were pulling for Vixen were taking their toll and she needed a good night's sleep. Preferably one that wasn't filled with lustful dreams of Cole.

"Time for an afternoon pick me up," Chloe sang, barging in without so much as pausing to knock.

Already full of energy, she bounced across the room and placed a cup of Starbucks Espresso Roast on the desk.

Olivia perked up, happy to indulge in a caffeine fix with her best friend. "Have I told you lately that I love you?"

"Not today, but you can do me one better." Chloe smirked, balancing on the edge of the chair across from Olivia's desk.

"Hmmm?" Sipping from the paper cup, she closed her eyes as the scalding liquid burned a path to her belly, warming her from the inside out.

"You still haven't told me if you're going to see Alex again. Spill! Right now, or I'm taking my coffee back."

Olivia's grip tightened protectively around the paper cup. "You are not getting this coffee back. Not even over my cold, dead body. And, no, I am not planning to see Alex again."

Shame ripped through her.

She'd called Alex Sunday night and given him the old 'it's not you, it's me' speech. He was a great guy, but there would never be anything between them. Much as she hated to admit it, he just wasn't Cole. Not that Chloe would understand since as far as she knew, things with Cole were one and done.

Thankfully, a knock at the door killed any further discussion of Alex.

Her jaw dropped at the sight of an outrageously large bouquet of long-stem roses and white calla lilies...on stilettos.

"These just arrived for you." Gabby peeked around the blossoms and stepped forward slowly, being careful not to spill any water on the carpet. "Should I just put them on your desk?"

"Holy crap!" Chloe blurted out, her gaze flying to the mammoth arrangement that nearly toppled Gabby.

"Uh, sure. The desk is fine." Olivia sprang to her feet and came around to help.

When they got the flowers settled on the desk, leaving zero work space, she thanked Gabby and turned her attention to the sweet-smelling new addition. She took a deep breath, inhaling the intoxicating scent of summer.

With oversized blossoms and crisp, vibrant colors, they were easily the most beautiful and extravagant flowers she had ever received, not that she was exactly accustomed to floral deliveries at the office.

Or anywhere else, for that matter.

And calla lilies just so happened to be her favorite flower. It was an incredibly sweet gesture, but who could have sent them? Clients didn't send gifts like this, no matter how much they appreciated her work. She tore the card from the bouquet and read it silently.

For a real Vixen.

Cole.

Desire stirred low in her belly, roaring to life at the very thought of his touch. She could resist his perfect smile, his cut abs, his sinful tongue. She could even handle his cocky I-can-make-you-come-whenever-I-want attitude. But this? What was this?

Naked friends—correction, *ex*-naked friends—didn't send flowers to each other, did they?

Maybe they did these days and she'd just missed the memo.

She *had* been out of action for a while.

"So, am I supposed to guess or are you going to tell me who they're from?" Chloe asked. She was trying hard to appear casual, but the mystery was probably killing her.

"There's no signature," Olivia told her, shrugging apologetically. It wasn't exactly a lie. She had her suspicions, but he hadn't signed his name, so how could she be sure? "I can't imagine who would have sent them."

She quickly tucked the card in her pocket, where it would be safe from curious eyes, including Chloe's. No way could she admit who they were from. People were already talking about her and Cole as if they were practically headed to the altar.

She wasn't ready to open that can of worms just yet. Or ever.

"And they say size doesn't matter," Chloe scoffed, flicking one of the roses with her pointer finger.

"This isn't funny."

"Tell me about it." Chloe flashed a devilish grin. "I can't remember the last time a guy sent me flowers."

"It's not like that," Olivia argued, rubbing her temples.

Whatever the flowers were, they meant something. Guys didn't just send a woman flowers without wanting something in return. She had a pretty good idea what that *something* was when it came to Cole.

Why couldn't he get it into his head that she couldn't just openly screw the boss?

"*Riiiight*," Chloe drawled, rolling her eyes. "There are only two reasons a man sends flowers like these—he's getting some action or he's *trying* to get some."

"Well, he can forget about it. My vagina is officially closed for business," Olivia swore, crossing her arms emphatically.

She was definitely not going to have sex with Cole again, no matter how big his *arrangement* was. Not even if he tried to lure her with those ridiculously gifted hands of his.

Or that mouth.

Nope. She was done with sex. At least for now. She just needed to set Cole straight.

Again.

She shooed Chloe out of her office and headed straight for Cole's, letting herself in without knocking and shutting the door behind her.

"Olivia—"

"Have you lost your mind?" she hissed through clenched teeth. She stalked across the office and placed her palms on the desk, leaning into his personal space. "You can't just send me roses at work!"

A smile tugged at the corner of his mouth and she knew he wanted to laugh. *Jerk.* And why did he have to be so sexy when he was being such an ass?

"Remind me again why I can't send you flowers?"

"Because," she sputtered, trying to remember why it was wrong. There seemed to be a sudden disconnect between her brain and her mouth. Probably had something to do with all the blood rushing to her center. "What will people think?"

"I sent you flowers; I didn't propose to you," he said, flashing her his trademarked dimpled grin. "And you're the one who pointed out people already think we're sleeping together. Why not run with it? You really need to loosen up." His smile turned seductive, his eyes hooding with desire. "I could help you with that, you know."

"And just what exactly did you hope to accomplish with this little stunt?" she demanded, doing her best to ignore the wicked glint in his gray eyes and the lock of dark hair that hung over his brow.

Her fingertips burned with the need to push the stray hair back and explore the softer side of the hardened man who sat in front of her.

"No hidden agenda. We're going to knock Vixen's socks off. Consider them a pre-closing celebration gift." He smirked at her and wiggled his eyebrows. "The post-closing could be even better."

"Cut the crap, Cole." She rolled her eyes, hoping he wouldn't see her flush with excitement at the thought of them celebrating the deal together. Alone. Naked. "I can't believe I have to reiterate this, but you can't send me flowers. I thought I was clear on that when I agreed to our little bargain." She straightened her back, placing a rebellious hand on her hip. "Which, by the way, was clearly a total mistake. No gestures. No public anything. Just a little secret sex."

Why was that so hard for him to understand?

And why did the words feel wrong when she said them?

"I told you the first time I met you—I get what I want." He crossed his arms stubbornly. The soft cotton of his blue dress shirt emphasized the broad muscles of his chest and shoulders, sending her focus into a tailspin once again. It was impossible to concentrate when all she could think about was the mind-blowing orgasms the man had given her.

"You're impossible!" she insisted, throwing her hands up in frustration.

She turned her back on him, fully expecting to get the last word, but he wasn't about to give up so easily.

"Olivia."

She paused at the door, her hand on the metal knob.

"You need to break things off with Wall Street."

She laughed and walked out, leaving the door open behind her. Go figure. They finally agreed on something.

34

OLIVIA

Olivia checked her watch for what felt like the hundredth time. She could still make it if she hurried. She walked a little faster, practically sprinting down the narrow hall in her four-inch heels.

The morning had been crazy busy and she had a million and one things to do, but she'd never forgive herself if she missed Jack's first solo pitch. The poor kid was probably a nervous wreck about presenting the Mama's Muffins campaign, especially after the big deal Cole had made of it, and she didn't want to abandon him.

The least she could do was show up for moral support.

Turning the corner to the conference room, Olivia slowed her pace and buttoned her jacket. She paused to catch her breath and slipped into the room as quietly as possible, not wanting to create an unnecessary distraction. Taking a seat in the back, she watched as Jack dove into the campaign.

With the Vixen pitch taking up every minute of her time, she had yet to review the final proposal for Mama's. She was anxious to see what the team had come up with, although she was certain they'd deliver. Despite Cole's initial reservations, she knew her team would pull it off.

They always did.

She could hardly believe her eyes as she watched Jack.

Was it her imagination or was he standing just a little bit taller today? Even his hair didn't look as unruly as usual. He was cool and confident, putting on a better show than she'd ever thought possible. What had happened to the meek, awkward kid who cracked at the first sign of pressure?

It was like watching *Invasion of the Body Snatchers* as he delivered the edgy 'Not Your Mama's Muffins' campaign. Not only had Jack's confidence gotten a boost, so had the campaign. The new campaign highlighted the delectable flavors and fillings that set Mama's apart from its franchised competitors and created a sexy, sinful eating experience.

Heck, by the time he was done, she wanted to take one of those muffins to bed.

She would never admit it to Cole, but he'd been right about taking a sexier approach with Mama's. And if she had to bet, the clients loved it too. Mama's sons were all smiles as Jack unveiled their new campaign.

Of course, what hot-blooded man wouldn't love seeing a beautiful woman lick muffin crumbs off her fingertips?

Jack wrapped the pitch up with surprising ease, getting approval to move the concept forward without any rework. She couldn't have been prouder of him. He'd come a long way in the last year. He still had a lot to learn, but he was becoming a more valuable part of the team with each campaign.

It wouldn't be long until Jack had a team of his own to coach.

She waited for the clients to leave before pulling him aside.

"You did a great job today," she told him, placing a hand on his shoulder. "You should be very proud of yourself. It's not often a client buys into the pitch on the first pass, let alone on the spot."

Jack blushed at the praise, his face and neck turning beet red. "Thanks."

"I also wanted to apologize for not being available to help more with this one." She grinned, pride swelling in her chest. "Not that you needed it, from what I saw today."

"No worries. I know you've been under a lot of pressure lately. Besides, I can't take all the credit," he admitted. He shifted nervously, and just like that, the old Jack was back. "Mr. Bennett actually helped me out."

"Cole? Helped you?" She didn't believe it.

First of all, the man lived to torment Jack, so why would he offer to help him?

Second, when could he have possibly found the time? They'd practically been attached at the hip lately and she hadn't even seen the final proposal.

"Yeah, I was a little surprised myself when he offered, but I'm not stupid." Jack laughed and tugged at his orange bowtie. "I knew I could use some pointers and he really helped me tighten up the pitch. It got me thinking..."

"Got you thinking what?"

"I probably shouldn't be saying this since he's the boss, but it made me realize I had pegged him all wrong. Sure, he likes to push people, but he's not so bad once you get to know him. He's really passionate about the business and he's got some original ideas. He could be really good for this place. You know, shake things up a bit."

"Perhaps," she agreed, "but don't forget that it was you who closed that deal today, not Cole. Take the rest of the afternoon off and go celebrate. You've earned it."

"Really?" Jack asked, perking up. "Thanks!"

He grabbed his laptop and made a quick exit, leaving Olivia alone with her racing thoughts.

She paced the room, wrapping her arms around her waist, as she tried to process everything Jack had told her. As usual, she didn't have much luck piecing together the incongruent pieces of the Cole Bennett puzzle.

Really, he had to be the most frustrating, confusing, impossible man on the face of the earth.

Every time she thought she had him figured out, he surprised her.

Never in a million years would she have believed he'd take time out of his busy schedule to help Jack. And yet he had.

While denial had become her new best friend, she had to admit that she'd misjudged Cole.

He wasn't just the arrogant asshat who strolled in, stole her partnership, and humiliated her team in front of her. He'd gone out of his way to help that very team find success. He'd sent her roses before their big pitch to boost her confidence. And then there was that night he'd swept her into his BMW and taken her home because of her migraine, and had bought her every breakfast food known to man the next morning to help her feel better. He had a sweet side she hadn't been willing to acknowledge before, and he seemed to have boundless confidence in her.

Was it possible Cole was a closet romantic?

It was too good to be true, wasn't it? Men like Cole didn't settle down.

And they didn't have hot one-night stands with strangers and then fall for them.

Cole dated models and actresses, and nobody for very long. If he wanted to date her—and she wasn't convinced that was the case, although she had to admit, it held a certain kind of appeal—what did that say about her?

35

COLE

Cole studied Olivia as she tapped furiously on the keyboard, putting the final touches on the Vixen proposal. She was completely focused on the task at hand and oblivious to his presence, but he didn't mind. He was just happy to be in her company.

Tomorrow they'd make the pitch and their late-night work sessions would come to a halt.

It wasn't exactly something he was looking forward to.

He'd grown to enjoy her sassy wit over the last few weeks and he was going to miss their time together.

He was especially going to miss the opportunities to see the flush in her cheeks when he looked at her and that fierce defiance that made her baby blues sparkle. Angry or excited or confused, Olivia was always gorgeous. She was smart as a whip, and it was clear why Pritchard had been thinking of her for partner before he arrived.

Yeah. He needed to do something about that.

It wasn't fair for Olivia to be killing herself as an associate when she was smarter than anyone else in the firm. Maybe even including him. If the pitch at Vixen went as well as he expected it to, maybe he could turn that to their advantage. If he could find a way to get Pritchard to make Olivia a partner, that solved a lot of problems.

She couldn't very well keep denying their connection by saying she couldn't sleep with her boss if they were at the same level. And he really didn't want to think that he'd seen the last of those killer legs wrapped around him.

"Ahem." Olivia was looking at him, gesturing toward the screen so he could see what she'd been working on. "You want to pay attention here for a second?"

"Yeah, sorry," Cole said, running a hand through his hair.

"Thank you," she said, a triumphant grin on her face, as she tucked a pen into her messy bun. "I think we're as ready as we're going to be. I'll walk you through it one more time and then I am going home to crash."

"Sounds like a plan," he agreed, glancing at his watch.

It was getting late and they both needed to get some sleep before tomorrow's meeting. If ever they needed to be on their A-game, tomorrow was the day.

They couldn't afford any mistakes.

Olivia quickly rolled through the slides, recapping the top-level talking points for him.

Not surprisingly, she had the whole damn presentation memorized.

When she was finished, she looked at him expectantly. "What do you think?"

"You've nailed it," he assured her, pleased with the latest changes and her ability to work so much of the market research into the deck. There would be no doubt they'd done their homework on the Vixen consumer and had created a campaign that would speak to her. The Vixen executives were going to love it. "Great work. You should be really proud of yourself."

"We should proud of ourselves," she corrected him, deflecting personal praise, as usual. "We did this as a team."

"Don't be so modest. In this city, modesty won't get you far," he advised. "Just say 'thank you' and take credit where it's due. You've earned it."

Olivia blushed, reminding him how uncomfortable she was being in the spotlight despite all her efforts to shine.

"Who'd have thought an Apple Butter Princess had it in her?" Cole teased, hoping to lighten the mood.

He knew she regretted telling him about her pageant days, but he had to give her a hard time about it every now and then. It was all in good fun. God knew he'd never have the courage to do something like that himself. Strutting around on stage and putting yourself out there for the sole purpose of being judged? Thanks, but no thanks.

As far as he was concerned, that took guts.

Still, if she ever found out about the hellacious garage band he started in high school, he'd never live it down.

"That's Apple *Blossom* Princess," she corrected him indignantly. The effect was ruined when she rolled her eyes and stuck out her tongue in a playful, un-Olivia-like gesture. "And don't you forget it!"

Before he could stop it, a deep belly laugh burst from him and soon she was laughing along with him, tears streaming down her face. Clearly they'd been working too hard and needed a good laugh.

And yet, it felt so right. Just the two of them having fun, sharing a silly joke.

"I never should have told you about my pageant days," she declared, clutching her sides as her laughter faded.

He wiggled his eyebrows. "Maybe if you're nice, someday I'll share the horrors of my own teenage days."

"I'm pretty sure I can guess what you were up to at the age of sixteen, and I'm not sure my innocent apple blossom ears can handle the sordid details," she retorted with a smirk, snapping her laptop shut and tucking it in her bag.

Cole's chest tightened.

He was really going to miss working so closely with Olivia. They'd see each other every day, but it wouldn't be the same. There was an unspoken sense of finality in the air tonight. And he was surprised to discover that he didn't like it one bit.

She pushed her chair away from the desk and rose to leave.

He grabbed her arm. Electricity flowed through him as their eyes met, the earlier levity forgotten. "Hey," he started, then hesitated.

What was he trying to tell her?

Olivia turned her blue eyes on him, her face looking puzzled. She chewed on her bottom lip. "Yes?" she asked.

It sounded like her voice trembled a bit, but Cole wasn't sure. Maybe he was just hearing what he wanted to hear.

"I just wanted to apologize. I was a dick to you at the beginning and it wasn't justified. I didn't realize when I started at PBA that I was taking something away from you." He paused. "You're really good at your job, Olivia. And we make a good team."

"We do." She nodded, shifting her weight and fidgeting with a stray lock of honey-blonde hair that had fallen loose from her bun. "Look, I owe you an apology, too. I was so angry when Jonathan brought in an outsider to do what I'd thought was my job that I lashed out at you before I even gave you a chance." She paused and shifted her weight again. "Anyway, I didn't get it then, but I understand why Jonathan brought you on. And I'm sorry we got off to such a rocky start."

"Olivia Masterson, are you saying we might be...friends?" Cole hung on that last word as he smiled at her.

Olivia flushed as her eyes settled on his and he realized just how vulnerable she really was, both physically and emotionally. This was the real Olivia. The one she kept hidden from the world. His heart hammered in his chest, both excited and unnerved to hear her answer.

A shaky grin spread slowly across her face. "Friends," she said at last.

He couldn't resist. He brought his hand to her face and rubbed his thumb across her bottom lip, smudging her lipstick. He had her in his sights and there was no escaping this time. "Friends with benefits?"

She stroked his cheek with her fingertips, sending a heatwave through his body. She leaned in closer to him, so close he could smell the summery scent of her perfume. "Don't push your luck," she murmured, her warm breath caressing his skin.

He pulled her close, sweeping his arms along her back, the fire in his belly spreading as his fingers explored her body. "Never."

He brought her mouth to his and kissed her fiercely, trying to drown out the nagging little voice at the back of his head.

You're totally unhinged. This isn't going to work.

He kissed her harder.

36

COLE

Olivia kicked off the Vixen pitch, speaking directly to Natalia Rodriguez, the president of Vixen Enterprises. Natalia was rumored to be a formidable woman who surrounded herself with strong women. Knowing that, Cole had suggested Olivia make the presentation, pitching woman to woman. They would take every subliminal, subconscious edge they could get and he would step in only if needed.

It was difficult for him to sit back and watch.

He was a hands-on kind of guy and liked controlling his own fate, but he also trusted Olivia. She knew what she was doing.

He watched with pride as she made the biggest pitch of her life.

Olivia was a force unto herself.

Ditching the glasses and letting her hair down, she'd finally embraced the feminine part of herself she'd worked so damn hard to bury. She exuded confidence, making her even more dynamic than usual. He realized he felt fortunate he'd found her in that bar, lucky to share even a tiny corner of her life.

Olivia was right: they were a good team. They worked damn well together, in bed and at work, and it looked like just maybe they might be able keep a good thing going. There were still so many things he didn't know, so much more to Olivia than the frigid Ice Queen who was all work and no play. Underneath that tough, businesslike exterior she hid a gentle, well-intentioned heart.

And that was part of what made her who she was.

Cole studied the faces of the Vixen executives.

They were enamored by Olivia. Setting the scene for them masterfully, she discussed the need to connect with real, working women, empowering them in their sexuality while also recognizing their societal contributions and familial obligations. She wove in details of the market research, laying the foundation for the daring conclusion.

As the pitch wound down, one of the women sitting at the table strode to the front of the room. The woman was rather average looking, nothing special. She could have been anyone; an executive, an admin, the girl who delivered the mail. Standing next to Olivia, she unzipped her jacket and revealed a racy Vixen bra. She flung the jacket over her shoulder, resting a hand on her hip and striking a traditional model's pose.

When she addressed the Vixen executives, her tone was commanding. "From the boardroom to the bedroom...be a vixen."

Another woman rose, following the lead of the first, and stripped off her shirt. "I'm a vixen."

And then a third. "Are you?"

Cole smiled. They'd pulled out all the stops, planting average models in the room in hopes of really driving the message home. Olivia had resisted at first, but he'd convinced her seeing the women make the transformation from working women to sexual beings live and in person would be more impactful than watching it on a screen.

He just hoped it would pay off. And that Pritchard didn't have a heart attack.

The old man looked like he was struggling for breath as he loosened his tie.

It had probably been a while since he'd seen a half-naked woman who wasn't his wife. Maybe they should've warned him, but it was much more fun this way.

"Genius," Natalia praised, clapping her hands together. "Well done, Ms. Masterson. This is the best pitch we've seen yet and I don't know that we'll see one better. This is exactly what we're looking for at Vixen Enterprises. You really got at the heart of what the Vixen brand is all about."

"Thank you," Olivia beamed, "but I can't take all the credit. Cole Bennett played a huge role in developing this campaign, as did many other associates at PBA. It really was a team effort. I'm so glad you're pleased with the result."

"Savvy and humble? A rare combination." Natalia swung a calculating gaze to Pritchard. "Watch out, Jonathan, I might have to steal this one away from you. I'm always looking for new talent."

"Don't even think about it," Jonathan waggled a finger at her. "The only way you're going to tap into Olivia is by signing a contract with PBA." He winked at Olivia.

"We still have two more agency meetings," Natalia informed him, "but I daresay we'll be back. I like what I saw today."

"We look forward to partnering with Vixen Enterprises," Cole told Natalia as he rose to shake her hand.

The woman had a firm grip, but he'd expected nothing less. She hadn't earned a reputation for being a shrewd business woman by being soft.

"That's right," Jonathan cut in. "You just let us know when you're ready to sign the paperwork and we'll have it drafted immediately."

When the meeting broke up, Cole signaled to Pritchard to walk with him. He'd catch up with Olivia later to congratulate her on an amazing performance. He couldn't have done it better himself.

Pritchard was his partner, but the man was a fool if he thought Olivia would be content with her current position for long. Natalia might have been smiling, but she was serious when she hinted at wooing Olivia away from the agency. And once word hit the street she had landed the Vixen account, Natalia wouldn't be the only one looking to wine and dine her.

Jonathan's best-kept secret was about to become one of the city's most sought after creative minds.

Cole had first-hand experience with colleagues he liked being wooed away from where he wanted them by job offers too tempting to resist. After all, that was had happened with Jacqueline in London. It hadn't really been her fault that a multi-million-dollar partnership offer trumped what he could offer.

People liked to talk about love and loyalty triumphing over all, but the real world didn't work that way.

However, if Olivia were to be offered a partnership at PBA, well, she'd have the job security she needed and could stop focusing so much on office gossip. The way he saw it, it was a win for everyone. Pritchard locked down an insanely talented employee, Olivia got the recognition she deserved, and he got to be the hero for once. He'd swept in and taken over the job she'd worked so hard for. It was only fair he set things right.

And if it also meant Olivia would finally have no excuses to reject their chemistry?

That was just icing on the cake.

37

OLIVIA

OLIVIA SKIMMED THROUGH HER EMAIL, jotting down notes on her 'to do' list, which was growing at an alarming pace with every scratch of the pen. A week had passed and there had been no word on the Vixen account, which meant she couldn't start any new projects. She'd be in limbo until the contract was awarded, one way or the other. And while she hated waiting for client feedback on a pitch, this lull was truly the calm before the storm.

If PBA got the Vixen contract, there would be a flurry of activity to get the campaign off the ground. Knowing that, she was using her down time to catch up on other projects and help out where the team needed her.

She was in the zone, reading story boards for the new Mama's Muffins commercial for the zillionth time and daydreaming about a nice long soak in the tub, when her phone rang. She scribbled a note to Jack and grabbed the handset.

"Olivia Masterson."

"Ms. Masterson? It's Gabby. Mr. Pritchard wants to see you as soon as possible."

Olivia's heart hammered in her chest. She hadn't heard

anything from Jonathan since the Vixen pitch. Come to think of it, she hadn't heard anything from Cole in a couple of days either.

Either this was very good news, or very, very bad news.

She let out a deep breath she hadn't realized she'd been holding. "Sure, Gabby. Tell him I'll be right there."

Olivia hung up the phone and sank into her chair.

Her limbs felt like Jell-O. She wondered if she should swing by Cole's office for a quick check-in. Maybe he knew what this was about.

No, she told herself firmly. If Jonathan had asked for her, then he wanted to see *her*.

She'd take her licks on her own like a grown-up.

She rose from her desk and smoothed her gray skirt. She'd bought this suit specifically for the Vixen pitch: it had just the right combination of sexy and sophisticated. That's what Cole had said, anyway.

She took one more deep breath and walked purposefully toward Jonathan's office.

Gabby waved her right in with a smile.

That was a good sign, right? Gabby wouldn't be smiling if she knew Olivia was about to get fired.

Olivia stopped to steel herself once more, staring at the heavy door. Somehow, meetings in Jonathan's office just never went quite the way she was hoping.

Squaring her shoulders, she straightened her back and strode into his office.

She felt herself relax when she saw it was just Jonathan waiting for her. She'd kind of expected Cole would be there too, but she was oddly relieved that he wasn't.

"Have a seat." He waved her toward the overstuffed leather chair.

Olivia's pulse was racing, her heartbeat thumping in her ears like a too-loud disco. She sat down, perched right at the edge of the chair.

"I have some news for you, Olivia," he began. He was positively beaming. That had to be good. "We've signed the Vixen account. Natalia Rodriguez told me herself that it was due to your excellent pitch."

Olivia felt every muscle in her body relax at once. The tension she'd been storing up all week literally melted away.

She sank back a little into the deep, soft chair. "That's fantastic news, Jonathan. Have you told Cole? He should be here. He was a big part of our team."

Jonathan smiled at her. He was really looking pleased with himself today, but Olivia couldn't blame him. Vixen was a *huge* account.

"Cole knows. Which brings me to the real reason I've asked you here." He folded his incredibly well-manicured hands in his lap, resting them on the soft gray silk of the suit that probably cost more than her first car. He was now positively grinning. "I'd like to make you a partner in PBA."

Olivia's stomach lurched. "I'm sorry, what?"

Jonathan continued smiling as nonchalantly as if he was describing what he'd eaten for breakfast that day. "Cole pointed out to me that I had been unfair to you by making him partner when I'd essentially promised it to you. He also pointed out that—"

"Excuse me, did you say *Cole* talked to you about this?" Olivia could hear herself slip straight into Ice Queen mode. She sat straight up in the chair, any thought of relaxation pushed out of her mind by what Jonathan was saying.

"Well, yes," Jonathan said. He hadn't caught on to Olivia's growing outrage, apparently, because he was still perched leaning on the edge of his desk, beaming like he'd had the best idea ever instead of, once again, ripping her damn dreams apart. "The Vixen pitch really emphasized the quality of your work, Olivia, and Cole argued that we'd be stupid not to secure your skills for our firm rather than let you be poached by the competition." He paused and looked at her. "Are you feeling well?"

Olivia was *not* feeling well.

She could feel the sweat seeping through her expensive silk blouse and plastering her hair to her neck. Her pulse roared in her ears.

She was confused.

She was nauseated.

And more than that, she was angry.

"I'm fine, thank you," she said, struggling to maintain her composure. She was damn well not going to run out of his office and throw up in the bathroom again, thank you very much. One time was more than enough. "It's just all rather unexpected. But I still don't understand what Cole Bennett has to do with this."

Jonathan nodded as a look of understanding spread across his face. "Ahh, I see. He didn't tell you. After the Vixen pitch, he lobbied quite hard for me to offer you this position. He seemed to think he owed it to you. If I didn't know your history better, I would think it was because he wanted to keep you around."

He winked at her.

Jonathan Pritchard had *winked* at her.

Shit.

This wasn't good.

This wasn't *fair*.

"I guess those late nights of teamwork had quite the effect on him," Jonathan said, still smiling like a perversely well-groomed Santa Claus. "He seems pretty taken with you. Not that I can blame him."

That was the last straw.

Olivia rose from the chair, her lips pressed into a tight imitation of a smile, and extended her hand to Jonathan. "Thank you for the offer, Jonathan. Really. I just need to think about it. It's been a big week for me."

Olivia turned on her heel and fled.

38

COLE

Cole was contemplating a stack of carryout menus his realtor had left when there was a sharp knock at the door. He tossed the menus in the drawer and glanced at the clock. He wasn't expecting anyone. Maybe this was one of those old-fashioned buildings where people actually believed in being neighborly. He was surprised to discover he didn't hate the idea as he made his way to the door. After all, this was home now.

The last thing he expected to find when he opened the door was Olivia standing there, wearing that little blue jacket that brought out her baby blue eyes.

The baby blue eyes that were currently sparkling with what appeared to be either intense arousal or rage. He *really* hoped it was the former.

"This is a surprise," he began, draping his arm over the door jamb. "I thought we were going ou—"

Olivia held up a hand. "Shut. Up."

Cole bristled. What was going on? Had she not heard about the Vixen deal yet?

Olivia tapped her foot. Her cheeks were flushed bright pink.

Yeah, this was definitely looking more like rage.

"Are you going to let me in? We need to talk."

He hesitated, wondering what could have possibly brought her to his door uninvited and unannounced. The silence between them was deafening as he studied her, the only sound the soft jazz floating down the hall from his living room.

Only one way to find out.

He stepped back and swung the door open for her. Without another word, he led her down the narrow hall, his bare feet moving silently over the rich mahogany floor. She was his first guest, and he wondered what she would think of the place as they emerged in the open concept loft space. He'd been shocked by the modern layout on his first tour. The building itself was ancient and had beautiful turn of the century character, but inside it was a completely different story. It was chic, modern, and surprisingly cozy.

Or had been, until Olivia had shown up royally pissed off about something.

He stopped at the couch and motioned for her to take a seat. "Make yourself comfortable."

Olivia sat, looking anything but comfortable.

"So how'd you find me, anyway? I just bought this place."

"I have my ways." Her voice was deadly quiet.

He'd never seen her quite like this before. When Olivia was angry, she was usually all spitfire and brimstone. God, it turned him on just thinking about the fiery encounters they'd had at work.

This, however, looked very different.

Cole sat down at the opposite end of the couch. "Do you want to tell me what's going on? I thought we were going out later to celebrate the Vixen deal."

Olivia's entire body stiffened. "I don't think I have a lot to celebrate right now," she said, her words hardened like her body.

"Would you mind explaining to me why Jonathan Pritchard offered me a partnership today?"

Cole relaxed a little.

He'd thought she'd had some bad news, but this was just a little matter of misunderstanding. He gave a little shrug and smiled at her. "I talked to him about it."

She stared at him, the wild fire in her eyes like nothing he'd ever seen there before. And wild as she looked in that moment, he suspected she was just getting warmed up.

Surely she couldn't actually be angry about this? She'd reminded him that the partnership should have been hers enough for him to know she'd wanted it.

A heavy silence hung in the air for a long moment before she spoke, enunciating the words too calmly for his comfort. "You told Jonathan Pritchard to give me a partnership. After I *told* you I don't want people interfering in my career. After I have told you *how many fucking times* that I need to earn my own way?"

Cole dropped his gaze, unable to look her in the eye.

How could he explain it? She was angry and maybe she had a right to be.

Hell, she probably did. He tried to imagine how he'd feel if their positions were reversed.

Olivia shook her head. Her hands were pressed firmly in her lap, her knuckles white. "Why? Why did you it, Cole?"

Cole couldn't think of anything to say, so he sat and said nothing.

"Was it so you could keep screwing me?" she spat, glaring daggers at him. "It was, wasn't it? Make me partner so you get to have sex with me, let me see, what were your words? *Whenever I want, without giving a damn?*"

"No!" he argued. She didn't really believe that, did she? After all the time they'd spent together, didn't she know him better than that? "I mean, I thought about that, too, but it wasn't the only reason, Olivia. I swear it wasn't."

"Was it because of Alex? You were such an asshole to him at the fundraiser, I knew you'd try and pull some sort of power play. I don't get you, Cole, I just don't." She slouched down into the couch cushions, her face now pale instead of flushed. "You don't want me to be with anyone else and you don't want to be with me, either. What do you want?"

What did he want? Cole didn't even know himself.

How could he tell her something he hadn't figured out even in his own fucked-up head?

He knew better than to commit to expressing his feelings before he understood the whole situation. That had only led to serious damage in the past.

"I don't know," he said. "I don't know."

Olivia shook her head. "How selfish can you be?" she asked, tears suddenly breaking free and streaking black streams of mascara down her cheeks with them. "Did you even think about what was best for me? Or was it all about what was best for *you*?"

Cole wanted to go to her, to comfort her, to take her in his arms and make her forget about all of this, but he didn't know what to say.

What could he possibly say to make her understand?

"Forget it. Your silence says it all," she said, sinking into the couch cushions again and covering her face with her hands.

"I felt bad," Cole said quietly, desperate to ease her pain and fix what he'd broken. Again. "I had no idea when I came to PBA that Pritchard was giving me your partnership. You earned it. I just wanted to make it up to you. Just calm down and listen to me for a second."

Shit. That was definitely the wrong thing to say.

Olivia jerked her gaze to his, her blue eyes hotter than a gas flame, her cheeks blazing red again. "*Calm down*? Are you fucking kidding me? How many times have I told you that people already think I'm some sort of corporate-ladder-climbing office bimbo who sleeps her way into promotions?" she yelled, each of her words like an angry blow to his chest. "And now you go and confirm that, again, by talking Jonathan into this hare-brained bullshit? How could you *possibly* think I could take it? That I would want it?"

"I just wanted to he—"

Olivia cut him off. "I never asked for your help. In fact, I thought I made it pretty damn clear that I didn't want it. Again, and again, and again! Just stop already! You don't get to decide for me. You don't get to decide where I work or who I sleep with or who I take on dates to stupid fucking fundraisers. I'm not some pawn in your little game you can shuffle around at will. I can't believe I trusted you. I thought you really cared about me, but you clearly don't know me at all."

Panic was beginning to set in. What was he supposed to say?

That he liked her? That he wanted to keep her around?

It didn't seem like anything he said would matter at this point.

"Just listen," he began, but Olivia held up her hand to stop him.

"I'm done listening," Olivia said, her voice soft. "I'm the only one who's been listening this whole time. It's clear you've never listened to me or what I want. I thought maybe we had something, that maybe if I would just open up a little we could even have more, but this is over. We're done."

She rose from the couch and smoothed her skirt, suddenly cool and dangerously collected. The Ice Queen again. The little gesture that he'd seen dozens of times broke his heart. Over? Done?

The idea of that hurt more than he'd thought possible.

39

OLIVIA

OLIVIA FIDGETED ON THE SOFT, buttery leather of the chair in Vixen's waiting area. "Thank you for agreeing to meet with me, Ms. Rodriguez," she muttered under her breath. "The reason I'm here today is—"

What exactly was she supposed to say? *I have to leave my job at PBA because I slept with my boss and then he pulled some strings to do me a favor that I didn't ask him for and now the entire freaking firm is convinced I'm the office slut they always thought I was?*

Probably not the most auspicious way to start a job interview.

Natalia's door swung open and Olivia rose to her feet, sucking in a deep breath.

Here goes nothing.

"Ms. Masterson." Natalia smiled, stepping through the doorway looking every bit the powerful executive. "It's so nice to see you again! I apologize for running late. Things have been rather busy with the spring fashion show just around the corner."

Olivia smiled and extended her hand. "No apology needed. I'm pleased to be here."

"Let's get down to business then, shall we?" Natalia gestured for Olivia to follow her into the office, which turned out to be nothing like Jonathan's.

Sure, Natalia had a bank of windows with a killer view of the city, but her walls were plastered with prints of Vixen campaigns and catalogue covers stemming back to the company's inception in the seventies.

Olivia admired the artwork, wondering what it must have been like to build such an iconic brand, blazing trails no other retailer dared. The women of Vixen were cutting edge and the new campaign would catapult the brand back to its rightful place at the forefront of the lingerie industry.

Natalia motioned to a sleek leather chair in front of her steel-and-glass desk and then sat down in a single, fluid movement. "So, Ms. Masterson, tell me why you're here."

Olivia swallowed hard.

She'd impressed Natalia and Vixen once before, right? She could handle this.

"First, please call me Olivia. I want to thank you for your kind words about our 'Be a Vixen' campaign. Jonathan told me you were impressed by our team."

"He should have told you that I was impressed by you, since that's what I actually said," Natalia said with a smile. "But why don't you cut to the chase, Olivia?"

Olivia's heart thudded in her chest. Her mouth felt suddenly dry. All those hours of practicing and her carefully prepared speech had flown out the window.

"I'm here because I want a job with Vixen," she said at last.

Natalia nodded but said nothing, just folded her hands together and placed them on the desk. Her gaze was almost as intense as Cole's, even if it didn't affect Olivia in quite the same ways.

"I realize your threat to steal me away from PBA during the pitch was a joke, but PBA is..." She paused for a moment. How exactly had she planned on saying it? "PBA and I have mutually decided that our futures lie in different directions."

Natalia let out a short laugh and shook her head. "Trouble with the boss?"

Olivia felt herself turn bright red. She knew she needed to say something, but there was some sort of twelve-pound watermelon in her throat keeping her words at bay.

Natalia waved her hand in a careless gesture of dismissal as she smiled at Olivia. "Men. They always think they know what's best for us. That they know what women want. And yet they are so rarely correct." She leaned forward and looked directly at Olivia. "I'm glad you're here, because I want you to work for me."

Olivia blinked rapidly but felt unable to move. "Really?"

Natalia laughed again. "Really. I've been looking for someone to lead my Marketing and Consumer Insights group. It's a new business unit for us, so you'd have complete freedom to build the department as you see fit, from the ground up. I think you're perfect for it. The research in your presentation was absolutely convincing, and I like your style."

Of all the ways Olivia had imagined this interview playing out in her head, she hadn't anticipated this one. It was radically different from her first interview with Pritchard five years ago. But then, she reminded herself, she'd been fresh out of college then, not a woman with years of experience in one of the best advertising firms around.

"I don't know what to say," Olivia replied. "It's an incredible opportunity and I'm flattered you'd consider me for the position. I'm just not sure I'm ready to lead a whole department."

"Nonsense," Natalia said. She leaned back in her chair and

studied Olivia, no doubt calculating her next words. "Modesty won't get you very far in this business, Olivia." Olivia's stomach lurched as she remembered that Cole had said exactly the same thing to her once. "Jonathan Pritchard doesn't hire incompetents. I know you led the team at PBA. Its loss is my gain. I fully expect you to be a good investment."

"I'm sorry, I just—"

Natalia raised her hand, silencing Olivia before she could finish her thought. "You came to me. Don't you think it's because you knew I'd say yes?" She fixed her clear, forceful gaze on Olivia and smiled. "I've seen your work. Sign on with Vixen Enterprises and you will get the recognition you deserve. The recognition that so far, you have not gotten."

Natalia's words hit the mark, slamming through her with the force of the cold, hard truth. If Pritchard truly valued her, she'd have Cole's job and she wouldn't be sitting here having this discussion in the first place.

Ugh. Cole. A wave of nausea rolled through her as she remembered their last terrible fight.

Natalia continued in her calm, steady voice, soothing Olivia's nerves back into submission. Olivia could see why she'd been so stunningly successful. "Vixen is a publicly held company whose board of directors is almost exclusively female. Women do well here without interference. You could also help lead other young women in need of a strong role model. That, my dear, has been one of my own greatest joys working at Vixen, and I believe it's something you would enjoy, too."

Olivia squared her shoulders and drew a calming breath.

She couldn't argue with Natalia's logic, and she really didn't want to.

Besides, she desperately needed to get away from Cole and the toxic mess that PBA had become for her since news of her "partnership" offer had been announced.

What was she waiting for? All she had to do was say yes.

An hour and a half later, she found herself on a whirlwind tour of the Vixen offices.

She matched the quick stride of her escort, nervous energy leaking from every pore on her body. Olivia smiled, drinking in the charged atmosphere of the busy office. It reminded her of her first walk through PBA. She'd been so young and hopeful and the office had seemed ripe with opportunity. Vixen had that same vibe and its own pool of bright eyed, young associates looking to make their mark in the city. Watching them, she could hardly believe how far she'd come.

Vice President. Not in a million years had she expected Natalia to offer her an executive position. It was a dream come true.

And she'd gotten the job without Cole's help.

40

COLE

Cole sat at his desk, arms crossed, trying to figure out where the hell he'd gone wrong.

Olivia's resignation sat in front of him, a glaring reminder that he'd royally fucked up.

Again.

She hadn't even bothered to tell him she was leaving. Jonathan had dropped that bomb, delivering a copy of the resignation letter himself. He hadn't been pleased. Not that he'd risk the Vixen contract over it.

No, that deal would close without a hitch.

PBA would make a hell of a lot of money, but they'd lose one of their brightest minds in the process. Filling her shoes wouldn't be easy. There was no one on the current team who was as experienced, dedicated, or creative as Olivia.

Her departure would leave a gaping hole at PBA.

And it was all his fault.

There wasn't a doubt in his mind that Olivia was leaving because of him.

She hadn't said it, but she didn't need to. Her actions spoke volumes. She hadn't uttered a single word to him since their last fight. Hadn't returned a single phone call, text, or even so much as looked at him in passing. As far as he could tell, she was ignoring his existence altogether.

And as much as he hated to admit it, it hurt like hell.

Maybe he should go to her? Try one last time to talk some sense into her?

She was packing up her office. It could very well be his last chance to plead his case. If he could just explain himself, maybe she'd understand. No, he'd make her understand. He was just trying to help. To make things right. To give her back what he'd unwittingly taken. What she deserved.

But would she even listen? It was unlikely.

Given their history, odds were they'd just end up in another knock-down, drag-out fight.

And he was already feeling shitty enough without making a spectacle of himself in front of the entire office.

He sighed and scrubbed a hand over his face.

As much as he wanted to go to her, to beg for her forgiveness, now wasn't the time. He needed to be patient, give her some time to cool off and let the dust settle. Then maybe they could try again, because no way was he just going to accept that they were over.

At least now they'd be on equal ground.

She wouldn't have to worry about office gossip and he wouldn't have to worry about getting nailed for screwing around in the office. As much as he hated to see her go, perhaps Olivia's leaving was for the best. She'd learn a lot working with Natalia and there would be no political baggage.

It would be a fresh start, something she clearly needed.

His gaze jerked to the hall.

Olivia. She was heading his way, looking as beautiful as ever with her honey-blonde hair fanned out over her shoulders. She stood tall, shoulders square as she made her way down the corridor. He waited with bated breath, hopeful she was coming to see him.

When she reached his office, she hooked a right without so much as glancing his way.

Cole's gut twisted. If that wasn't a big 'fuck you', he didn't know what was.

They were over. He was completely, totally, one hundred percent certain of it.

Olivia had meant it when she said she was done with him. She wouldn't be coming back and there wasn't a damn thing he could do about it.

41

OLIVIA

"Love sucks," Olivia muttered, talking to herself as she tried, and failed miserably, to weed through resumes for her new team. She was doing her best to throw herself into her work as she'd always done, but it was a struggle.

She couldn't stop thinking about Cole.

It wasn't fair. She'd turned in her notice at PBA and stalked proudly past Cole's office, not giving him a single glance. She loved her new job as director of Marketing and Consumer Insights at Vixen Enterprises. She was working for someone who respected her, who wouldn't try to seduce her or interfere in her career.

So then why did she feel like shit?

Cole's actions had been beyond the pale, certainly. How many times had she told him that she just wanted to make it on her own, without somebody else swooping in to mistakenly save the day? And yet he'd refused to listen every time, convinced that he knew her needs better than she did.

Except, at least when it came to the needs that spiraled through her body every freaking time she thought about Cole, he kind of *did* know her needs better than she did.

But that was the problem, she reasoned. Sure, they were good in bed together.

Scratch that; they were *great*.

She couldn't deny the immense pleasure he was capable of giving her with even a flick of his fingertip. But he couldn't seem to understand her point of view about the really important things. Didn't even seem to want to. She'd been a fool to think they could have had anything other than an insanely intense physical connection.

Of course, she'd miss that.

She missed his strong arms wrapping around her, pulling her close to him. She missed his kisses. She even missed their playful bickering.

But he'd ruined everything.

Every time she thought about how casually he'd talked about getting her the partnership at PBA, her blood boiled. He'd lied to her. How could she trust him when he'd purposefully gone behind her back and manipulated her career? How could he not have understood what that would do to her reputation at the firm? If he'd truly been looking out for her best interests, he never would have interfered. He would have respected her independence instead of using their relationship to give her a hand up.

She had to remind herself of that, or she'd go and do something stupid like forgive him.

Her assistant Greer came to her door holding a binder.

Olivia cursed again under her breath, and Greer turned on her stiletto heel and left without a word. Leaning back in her chair, Olivia closed her eyes. What she just needed was a few minutes to collect herself.

She sat like that for a while, unaware of how much time had passed until her phone vibrated.

Glancing at the screen, she saw a text from Chloe.

Guilt tore through her like white hot lightning. She'd been avoiding Chloe, unable to give voice to her pain and talk about things with Cole. It was just too much.

Curiosity finally got the best of her and she reached for the phone. She swiped the screen and read the message: *Cole hasn't been to work in two days!*

Good, she typed without hesitation. At least she wasn't the only one feeling like utter shit.

Her phone buzzed again almost immediately. She read Chloe's newest message and sighed. *What's going on?!? CALL ME.*

She'd call Chloe later, but first she had to get through these resumes.

With renewed focus, she plowed through the stack, sorting them into potential candidates and File 13. Despite the large applicant pool, there were only a half-dozen or so who were truly qualified and warranted interviews.

She scribbled a note to Greer with instructions for scheduling the interviews with potentials and took the rest to the shredder. As the machine whirred the pages into oblivion, her thoughts drifted back to Cole.

To his sterling silver eyes.

To the dark hair that always dropped into his eyes.

To the way he'd smiled at her across her breakfast bar in her lonely little apartment.

She couldn't have imagined it *all*, right? He had to have felt *something*. Even if it hadn't ended up being enough.

"Girl, what are you doing here so late?" Natalia's voice snapped her back to reality.

"Just finishing up those resumes," she explained, forcing a smile. "There are some great candidates. With any luck we'll be up and running in a few weeks."

"So what's the problem then?" Natalia crossed her arms, the

look of concern on her face worthy of Olivia's own mother. "You've been moping around here all week."

"Everything is—"

"Stop," Natalia commanded with a flourish of her hand. She strode across the room and slipped gracefully into one of the chairs opposite the desk, looking every bit the powerhouse executive in her crimson suit. "I realize we don't know each other that well yet, and it's going to take time for us to get to a level of trust where we can be brutally honest with one another, but girl, you look like someone just ran over your puppy. So how about we just skip all the B.S. and you tell me what's bothering you? I'm a pretty good listener."

Olivia contemplated Natalia's offer. She couldn't possibly explain the messy situation with Cole. She wasn't even sure what the situation was herself.

Correction: what the situation had been. It was definitely nothing now.

"Besides," Natalia prompted with a spirited grin, "tomorrow is our biggest fashion show of the year, and I can't have people thinking that long face of yours comes from working here. How would that look?"

Olivia sighed. "I'm just upset about what happened at PBA. Cole pulled strings behind my back to get Jonathan to offer me that partnership, even though he knew it would make people talk. He didn't care. He just did what he wanted to do so I would sleep with him again."

Natalia leaned back in her chair, studying Olivia.

It was hard to read her body language and she had no idea what the other woman was thinking.

"I've known Cole Bennett for a long time," Natalia finally said. "He doesn't invest easily. I understand that his interference irritates you. It would irritate me too, frankly. But don't be too hard on the guy." Natalia stood and smoothed her jacket. "I think you know as well as I do that if all Cole had wanted from you was sex, he'd have gotten it without going to such lengths." She pulled two all-access passes for the fashion show from her pocket and tossed them on the desk. "Now chin up, sweetheart. You've got work to do tomorrow. Try and look happy. You're a Vixen now."

42

COLE

COLE GROANED, cursing the pounding in his skull. He felt around blindly and found a pillow, which he pulled down over his head. It didn't help.

Would the incessant pounding never stop?

He promised himself he'd never touch a bottle of Scotch again if it would just go away.

When it finally subsided, he sighed with relief, but his relief was short lived.

The living room blinds were thrown open, the harsh light of the morning sun blinding him in his hung-over state.

"What the fuck?" he mumbled as the bottle of Scotch was snatched from his grip.

"What the fuck is right," Anna replied, hand on her hip. Cole brought a hand up to shield his eyes from the morning sun. It didn't help. In fact, it seemed highly possible his skull would crack open at any second, which might actually be a blessing compared to the alternative. With the sun at her back, Anna looked like a tiny Amazon warrior ready to kick his ass. "You look like hell."

"Thanks," Cole muttered, dragging himself to a sitting

position. He scrubbed a hand over his face, getting a not so gentle reminder that he needed to shave. "Remind me again why I gave you a key?"

"For emergencies, obviously."

"I hardly think this qualifies as an emergency." Cole groaned and buried his face in the couch pillows. If this was Anna's idea of emergency care, he was getting that key back before she left today. "Can you please close those blinds? You're killing me here."

"The pain is good for you," she replied from the kitchen where she was pouring his last bottle of Johnnie Walker Black down the drain. "It reminds you that you're alive. Do you even know what day it is?"

"The better question would be, do I care what day it is?"

Anna returned to the living room, sitting on the coffee table in front of Cole. She twisted the top off a bottle of water and handed it to him along with two aspirins he desperately needed.

"What's going on? You haven't returned a single one of my calls this week. I was worried about you."

"I'm fine," he lied, knowing full well Anna would never believe him given his present condition. "Just taking a few personal days. People do that, you know. Take time off."

"You are quite obviously not fine." Anna gestured around the room, which was littered with takeout containers and empty liquor bottles. In the light of day, he could see the whole place was a disaster. Hell, he was a disaster. "What in the hell happened to you?"

"Olivia Masterson happened," Cole groaned.

"Who?" Anna shot him a concerned look. "Start at the beginning and tell me what happened, Cole."

So he did. He told her about how they'd instantly connected (leaving out, of course, some of the sister-inappropriate details). How Olivia would never really let him in because she was afraid of the damage to her reputation. How he'd tried to fix everything by talking to Pritchard about getting her the partnership she deserved.

Anna held up a hand in surprise. "Hold on. You did what?"

Cole shrugged. "I talked to Pritchard about making Olivia partner. It made sense. She'd done such great work with the campaign, and it was my fault she didn't get it in the first place. And then after all that she just ditched me for a job at Vixen."

Anna shook her head. "So this Olivia repeatedly tells you how important it is to her for her succeed on her own, and you go behind her back to pull strings? Good lord, big brother, I'd have bailed too. What were you thinking?"

"That's not fair," Cole retorted. "I tried to talk to her. I tried to explain I was just doing this because I wanted her to be happy, and she wouldn't listen. She just kept insisting that I was only doing it to get her back in the sack."

"And do you think the reason Olivia got the wrong impression about your motivations is because you weren't man enough to tell her the honest truth, which is that you're *clearly* in love with her?"

Damn. Anna never had been one to mince words, but she'd morphed into a tiny drill sergeant perched on his coffee table.

"I never said I was in love with her," he said, scowling.

"You didn't have to." Anna gestured to the empty liquor bottles strewn across the room. "The only time I've ever known you to try and drink yourself half to death is when your heart's been broken."

"It wouldn't have mattered anyway." He leaned forward, resting his elbows on his knees and buried his face in his hands. "Just like it didn't matter the last time."

"This isn't a Jacqueline situation," Anna stated, unfazed. "*Jacqueline* didn't leave you for another job because you were a controlling dick who went behind her back and pulled strings she explicitly told you not to pull. Jacqueline left because she wasn't in love with you and didn't want what you wanted. I'm sorry, I know that hurts to hear, but it's true. And you have never wanted to own up to your emotions since then, and that is what's gotten you in this situation."

Cole scrubbed his face with his hands.

Anna was right. He hadn't been the same since London. He'd put up walls to defend himself from ever feeling hurt again the way he'd been hurt then. And now those walls were responsible for driving Olivia away.

He couldn't forget how she'd looked at him that last night, like he was something foul that needed to be scraped off the bottom of her shoe.

Then, it had hurt his pride. Now, it just hurt.

"So, you've screwed up big time," Anna stated matter-of-factly. "What are you planning to do about it?"

"Do about it?" Cole felt like a kid learning to read, repeating things he didn't seem to understand. "I don't think better late than never really applies here, Anna. I don't know if there's anything I *can* do."

"Well, sitting here feeling sorry for yourself is definitely not going to fix anything," she pointed out, crossing her arms across her chest. "I'm not letting you give up on this girl, Cole." She crossed her legs and bounced her foot mindlessly, seemingly lost in thought. "You're gonna need to make a grand gesture."

"I don't even know what that means."

"Of course you don't," she replied, rolling her eyes. "That's why you're in this situation. Haven't you seen *any* movies? You need to man up, admit you were a *total* asshat, and tell this woman you're crazy about her and you can't live without her."

He cringed and pinched the bridge of his nose.

"In public," she added. "You embarrassed her publicly. It's

only fair. And, Cole? It'll have to be big. A dozen roses isn't going to fix this mess."

If he didn't know better, he'd have thought she was enjoying putting him in his place. After all, wasn't she the one who'd wished true love and happiness on him in the first place?

43

OLIVIA

OLIVIA STARED at the fashion show passes, trying to decide what to do with the second one. Natalia's suggestion was hardly subliminal, but that didn't mean she had to take it. She could do whatever she wanted with the pass, and while it was easy for an outsider to suggest she should forgive and forget, it just wasn't that simple.

It would never be that simple. Not with Cole.

Steeling her resolve, Olivia grabbed her phone and dialed.

It was time to stop living in her head with worry and regret. She'd spent too much time there lately. It was time to get back to the real world.

Thankfully, Chloe answered on the first ring.

"It's about time," she barked. "What the hell is going on with you? You just left your job and didn't even tell me what happened."

"I'm sorry," Olivia said, shifting uncomfortably in her chair. She deserved the tongue-lashing Chloe was likely to give her, but that didn't mean she had to like it. "I should have called sooner. I just... I just wasn't ready to talk about it yet."

"Cole?" Chloe asked, her words softer and swathed in empathy.

If anyone could sympathize with a broken heart, it would be Chloe. She'd had more than her fair share. The difference was, she hadn't given up on finding true love.

"Cole," she admitted, her broken heart aching at the mention of his name. She'd have to work on that.

"Tell me everything."

So she spilled her guts, telling her best friend how she'd thought maybe, just *maybe* Cole had had feelings for her, and then how he'd gone behind her back and proved she was an idiot for imagining he could have wanted anything but the obvious.

"I'm going to kick his ass!" Chloe shouted with enough conviction that Olivia experienced momentary concern for Cole's physical wellbeing.

"I don't think that will actually help."

"I don't care if it helps," Chloe argued. "He clearly needs a good ass kicking to get his head on straight. What was he thinking?"

"Who knows?" She sighed. "It doesn't matter. What's done is done. And while I appreciate the offer, I'd rather not think about you sharing a cellblock with New York's finest. I have enough to worry about right now."

"Fine," Chloe said. "What if I just drop a little Ex-Lax in his morning coffee?"

"Chloe..."

"Well, I can't just sit here idly! There must be something I can do to help. I feel sort of responsible since I made the dare in the first place. Not to mention, I told him about your lust for lilies."

Olivia swallowed a lump in her throat.

The flowers. She'd forgotten the flowers he'd sent just before the Vixen pitch. *For a real Vixen*. He'd asked Chloe about the lilies.

She had to stop thinking about him.

"I was so sure he was going to be the one. I can't believe he fooled me," Chloe said. "What a schmuck!"

"Don't be so hard on yourself. He fooled both of us." It was hard for her to accept that she'd been played for the fool. Again. She was a smart woman. So why hadn't she seen his betrayal coming? Maybe she needed a coach. They had fashion coaches and weight loss coaches and even life coaches. Surely she could find someone to keep a watch out for dirty, underhanded backstabbers? Olivia shook her head, clearing her thoughts. "Actually, there is something you could do for me."

"Anything," Chloe said without hesitation. "It sounds like I owe you one."

"Will you be my date for the Vixen fashion show tomorrow? I know it's short notice, but I've got an extra ticket and I really don't feel like going alone."

"Really?" Chloe squealed. There was a loud bang and Olivia was certain she'd dropped the phone in her excitement. When she returned, she rushed on. "I'd love to. Just one question. What should I wear?"

44

OLIVIA

OLIVIA SKIRTED her way through the sea of bodies, searching fruitlessly for Chloe.

Where on earth could she have gone?

She prayed Chloe hadn't snuck backstage for an early preview while she'd been busy with Natalia. Olivia had been at it for the last hour, shaking hands, making polite conversation and basically torturing the hell out of her feet in a pair of too-tight Jimmy Choos that desperately needed to be broken in. Fortunately, Chloe was a social butterfly and perfectly comfortable making the rounds on her own while she did the work thing.

If the energy in the room was any indication, the show was going to be a huge success.

She couldn't recall the last time she'd been in such a charged environment.

Of course, she didn't make it a habit of frequenting the fashion scene, but the excitement in the air was nearly palpable as the crowd speculated on the new Vixen designs. Natalia had worked the crowd like a pro, teasing them into a frenzy without giving anything away. Even Olivia had been swept up in the excitement.

For the first time in days, she was starting to feel like her old self.

Spotting Chloe, she grabbed two champagne flutes from a passing server and made a beeline for her friend. The show would be starting soon and she wanted to claim their seats along the runway before some overly eager fashion blogger snagged them.

Besides, her feet were screaming for mercy.

"Having fun?" she asked as she handed Chloe a glass.

"The. Most." Chloe laughed appreciatively and sipped her champagne. "I've never been to a fashion show before. This is ridiculous! There are so many people. And all these lights!" she cooed, spinning to admire the lights that cut across the crowd, never stopping and continuously moving and shifting.

"Tell me about it," she agreed. "The show will be starting soon. We should probably find our seats. We're on the right side of the runway. Front row."

"Front row?" Chloe squealed.

"This job does have its perks," she teased, weaving her arm through Chloe's and linking elbows.

"Have I told you I *love* your new job?"

Olivia rolled her eyes, steering Chloe toward their reserved seats. "You may have mentioned it once or twice."

The lights flashed briefly as they settled into their chairs, signaling the crowd to be seated.

She smiled and checked her watch.

Natalia had warned her the show wasn't likely to start on time and she'd been right. No surprise there. She scanned the crowd, nodding to a few of her coworkers as they waited.

A hush fell over the crowd as the lights died down and the runway came to life.

Spotlights danced across the stage, keeping time with the loud techno music pumping through the speakers. She snuck a quick peek at Chloe who was awestruck. It was hard to blame her. The videos she had watched of prior Vixen shows clearly hadn't done justice to the real deal. The music pulsed through her body, making it impossible not to get caught up in the mood.

When Natalia finally stepped onto the runway, the crowd was silent.

She gave a brief introduction to the fall line, her usual wit and charm winning the crowd over. By the time she was finished, they were eating out of the palm of her hand and Olivia had no doubt orders would be pouring in from the select group of buyers who'd been invited to attend the show.

The DJ cranked the music up as the models began strutting down the runway in some of the sexiest lingerie she had ever seen.

"Oh my god," Chloe whispered, eyeing a lacey gold bustier and matching panties. "I'm in love. Look at those undies! They are killer! Please tell me you negotiated free samples as part of your compensation package?"

"I'll see what I can do," Olivia promised.

After all, it wasn't like she'd be in need of sexy underwear any time soon.

"Seriously, Liv. This job is so much cooler than working at PBA. You are so lucky!" Chloe swore. "Well, I guess it wasn't luck so much as hard work, but you know what I mean."

The rest of the show passed in a blur as they whispered about their favorite pieces and how great the models looked.

By the time Natalia returned to the stage, she was grateful for the reprieve from the earsplitting music.

"Thank you all for coming tonight," Natalia started, smiling warmly at the massive crowd. "Once again our designers have outdone themselves, delivering an amazing collection guaranteed to bring your inner vixen roaring to life. Please join me in giving these lovely ladies another round of applause!"

The models paraded back onto the runway amid thundering applause, reminding her fleetingly of her own time in the spotlight. The women fanned out on the runway, as Natalia started her closing remarks.

"Spring has always been my favorite time of year. And not just because it means the launch of fabulous new Vixen lingerie," she teased, winking at the crowd. "I may be a hopeless romantic, but for me spring always brings with it the promise of new love, new beginnings and, of course, new lingerie. At Vixen, we believe anything is possible when love is in the air, which is why I've invited a dear friend of mine to join me on stage today. This is his first time on the runway and he's a little nervous, so be gentle!"

The spotlight shifted from Natalia, settling on a tuxedo at the back of the stage.

As the suit stepped from the shadows and into the bright light, revealing the face of the man wearing it, Olivia nearly fell off her chair.

"You didn't tell me Cole was going to be part of the show," Chloe whispered, raising a questioning eyebrow. "Did you know about this?"

She shook her head in reply, completely speechless. What *was* Cole doing onstage?

It was too soon to reveal the new campaign. It wasn't ready. So what then?

He walked down the runway, looking nervous and completely out of his element.

The usually cool and confident Cole Bennett clutched his microphone in two hands as if it were a lifeline and he was two seconds from becoming shark bait. As he closed the distance between them, anxiety pierced her calm, reminding her of the pain he'd caused. She was also reminded of how much she missed him and how good they'd been together.

While it lasted.

"Good evening," he began, giving the crowd one of his dimpled smiles and no doubt melting a few panties in the process. "My name is Cole Bennett, and I guess you could say I'm a bit of a runway virgin. The truth is, I'm probably in over my head today."

The audience laughed good naturedly. How could they not? The man was a natural born charmer.

And he looked damn good in that tux.

"Actually, I've been in over my head for a while now. I was just too blind to see it. I thought I had the world all figured out, that I was in complete control. Great job. Beautiful women. The right zip code," he finished, ticking them off on his fingers wistfully. "I was flying high and nothing was going to drag me down. Nothing, it turns out, except my ego."

Olivia's heart began to race. Surely not. Was he really? Could he be?

"I was a superficial prick. I got burned once, and because of that I shut everyone out, never letting anyone get too close. And when I finally met a woman who made it past my defenses, I wasn't honest with her, and I wasn't honest with myself. I didn't listen to what she wanted, and as a result I did everything wrong. And I mean *everything*."

Once again, laughter rippled through the crowd.

Olivia's hand flew to her mouth. She couldn't believe her ears. Cole was actually confessing to a crowd full of strangers. This was either the most romantic or most desperate thing she'd ever seen.

The jury was still out.

"Oh my god, Liv," Chloe blurted out as a second spotlight dropped from the ceiling and landed on Olivia, setting her cheeks on fire. "He's talking about you!"

"Shh!" she shushed her friend, not wanting to miss a word. This moment was going to be seared into her brain for all time.

Cole searched the crowd, his eyes locking on Olivia, drilling her with a passion beyond anything she'd ever experienced. Her stomach twisted in knots. How the hell did he do that?

"I didn't know the first thing about being in a relationship. I thought I could control the world around me, and in my hubris, I lost sight of what was really important," he explained, speaking directly to her now, the rest of the crowd forgotten as he delivered his heartfelt apology. The one she'd been doing her damndest to avoid. The one that had the potential to be lethal to her resolve. "While I wanted nothing more than to be your partner—*your equal*—my actions sent a different message. I know now that being in a relationship isn't about having control, it's about giving it up. I was stupid and thoughtless and I broke your trust, Olivia. The trust of an incredible, intelligent, driven woman—the only woman I've ever loved."

She gripped the edge of her seat, her knuckles going white.

It was all happening so fast. She couldn't process.

Ten minutes ago she'd been trying to figure out how to wrangle Chloe a pair of gold undies and now this?

"Love?" she whispered, knowing full well he couldn't hear her, despite the eerie silence that had fallen over the crowd.

Cole jumped down from the runway, landing gracefully as though stage hopping were an everyday occurrence for him. He laid his microphone on the edge of the runway, next to the stiletto clad foot of a teary-eyed model, and spun to face her. He grasped her hands, wrapping them in his warmth, and pulled her to her feet.

Olivia stood on wobbly knees, praying her legs would hold up.

The last thing she needed was a face plant in front of an audience this large.

Not exactly how she imaged her Vixen debut.

Of course, she hadn't quite imagined this scenario either, so she was in uncharted waters all around. Still, Cole *loved* her! And he'd just waxed poet about her *brains*! Unable to stop the grin that spread across her face, she basked in the admission, letting the knowledge warm her from the inside out.

"I love you, Olivia. I was so scared to admit it to myself that I drove you away. I don't deserve a second chance," he said, squeezing her hands and sending warm fuzzies straight to her heart, melting the frost she'd allowed to accumulate. "But if you give it to me, I'll prove you made the right choice."

Cole dropped to one knee, his eyes taking on a glassy sheen.

Olivia was tearing up herself. Her pulse thundered in her ears as she fought a losing battle. She was drowning in quicksilver and sinking fast. It was inevitable, she supposed. The man she loved was on his knees begging for forgiveness.

And she wanted to forgive him. She truly did.

But, could she trust him?

She couldn't bear to be disappointed again. She couldn't go through that hurt even one more time. She was maxed out on bending, she'd surely break next time.

"Cole, I—"

"Say yes!" someone yelled from deep within the crowd.

"Liv?" Chloe prompted. "I don't want to rush you here, but if you don't say yes soon, one of these other ladies is going to snatch that man right up."

Olivia looked deep into Cole's gray eyes, searching his soul for the future she so desperately wanted. Beyond the unshed tears she saw compassion, respect, and most importantly, love.

Neither of them was perfect, but maybe together they could be.

Cole had put himself out there, laying his soul bare in front of hundreds of strangers, finally admitting that he was wrong to interfere with her career, and declaring that he was in love with her. Her brains, as well as her body. *Her.* So what was she waiting for? Happily ever after was staring her in the eye.

She just had to be brave enough to open her heart and take a chance.

"I love you, too," she declared, finding her voice strong and sure despite the swell of emotion, "but get off that knee or people are going to get the wrong idea! You've got one more chance, Cole Bennett. Make it count."

He leapt to his feet, sweeping Olivia up in his arms and spinning her around as she crushed her mouth to his. Their lips melded together as if they'd never been apart, reaffirming her decision to give their love a shot. They'd make it work this time. She knew it from her racing heart, to her throbbing pelvis, right down to the tips of her curled toes.

If she was going to open her heart and take a chance on love —the messy, screwed up, beautiful kind—it had to be with Cole. She couldn't imagine a future that didn't include his arms wrapped around her. His tongue slipped between her lips, charging her body like a live wire. She hardly noticed when the audience burst into raucous applause.

She was too busy making up for lost time.

"I think they approve," he laughed breathlessly when the kiss finally ended. "Want to get out of here?"

"I thought you'd never ask," she replied, a hot flush creeping up the back of her neck as she thought about the hundreds of eyes watching them play tonsil hockey. She turned to Chloe.

"Get out of here already," she said, waving a hand nonchalantly. "I'll get a cab."

"Thanks, Chloe. Enjoy the rest of your evening." Cole flashed her one of his smiles and dropped his lips to Olivia's ear. "I've got a car outside."

"You know," she whispered, snaking her arm around his waist. "I've always wanted to do it in a limo."

45

COLE

WHEN THE DRIVER closed the door, giving them total privacy, Cole pulled Olivia onto his lap. Now that he finally had her back in his arms, he wasn't about to let her go. She straddled him, looking flushed and incredibly sexy, as she ground her hips against him. The friction of the act brought his cock to full attention as it sought release deep within the wet heat of the woman he loved.

"Please tell me it's laundry day." He slipped a hand under her flowing skirt. *Damn.* His fingers skimmed over a pair of barely there lace, string bikinis. "How attached are you to these?" he asked, tugging on the restrictive undergarments.

"I work for a lingerie company now, remember?" She grinned. "They're easily replaced."

"Glad to hear it because they've got to go if I'm going to make that fantasy of yours come true."

"And what fantasy is that?"

"The one where I make you come in less than twelve blocks."

He reached under her skirt and ripped the thin fabric with one firm tug. His thumb found its way to her center, gently massaging her clit as she pumped her hips against him, head thrown back, hair cascading over her shoulder in golden waves.

Damn she was beautiful. And wet.

He would never get tired of this. Seeing her let go and give herself over to him, to the bond they shared.

"Aren't you a little overdressed for a fashion show?" Olivia panted.

"I figured if I was going to crash and burn, I might as well look good doing it," he explained, placing a kiss on her exposed collarbone and working his way up her neckline.

Her skin was hot to the touch. She was burning up. *They* were burning up.

All was right in the world.

"I'd say you succeeded," she teased, unbuttoning his pants with swift fingers. She released his cock and stroked it, sending shockwaves through his body. "Baby, I need you inside me now."

He groaned in ecstasy as she lowered herself onto his shaft in one quick motion, her body clenching him tightly and claiming him as her own. "I've missed you so much."

"I see that," she purred, rocking her hips slowly and taking him deep. If he didn't know better, he'd think she was testing his endurance. Fortunately, it was a short ride back to his apartment and he meant to make good on his promise. They'd both come before this ride was over. They had the rest of their lives to take it slow. "Don't think this means you're off the hook, Cole Bennett. You still have a lot of making up to do."

"Sweetheart, I'm just getting started," he promised, gripping her hips and lifting his pelvis to her, matching her feverish pace as she pushed them toward climax.

"Now that's what I'm talking about."

She lowered her mouth to his, placing a gentle kiss on his lips before pulling back. She was definitely teasing him now, challenging him.

He knew just how to respond.

When she leaned in for another kiss, her nose just a hair's breadth from his, Cole twisted his fingers in her hair, tilting her head to the side and taking control. As expected, his aggression fueled her passion, her kisses becoming deeper and more desperate as her tongue sought refuge in his mouth, mating with his own.

He said a silent prayer for second chances.

If Olivia had rejected his apology, well, he couldn't even think about it. The prospect of going through the rest of his life without moments like this, without holding her close, was unfathomable. He would be true to his word, and when the time was right, he'd make her his wife, if she'd have him.

"Baby, you've only got a few more blocks to pull this fantasy off," she chided, panting as she rode Cole to ecstasy, their bodies crashing together in harmony.

"That sounds like a challenge."

He smirked, slipping a hand between them to massage the bundle of nerves he knew would push her to oblivion. He rolled his thumb across her center as she rocked her hips furiously, clutching his shoulder and digging her nails into the soft fabric of his jacket. He leaned back, riding the ascent to his own orgasm as her body drew him toward climax.

Just two more quick strokes and Olivia's moans reached a crescendo the driver was sure to have heard, her body tightening around him, demanding he join her in a shattering release the intensity of which he'd never experienced before. His body shuddered with pleasure as she withdrew everything he had to give.

When she finally collapsed on his chest in exhaustion, he held her tight, stroking her hair and planting a kiss on top of her head. What he wouldn't give to extend the ride, even by a moment, so he wouldn't have to let her go. This was what it was all about, the quiet moments with the one you loved.

It had taken him a while, thirty-four years to be exact, but he finally understood.

"That. Was. Amazing," she declared, sitting up and zipping his pants. Her eyes were bright and her smile was as wide as he'd ever seen. She truly was the most beautiful woman in the world. "We have to do this again."

"Your wish is my command."

Olivia threw her head back and laughed. "I'm going to hold you to that, you know."

"I'd expect nothing less," he admitted, grasping her hands in his once again. "I meant everything I said tonight. I am going to spend every day for the rest of my life doing whatever it takes to make you happy."

"Whatever it takes?" she asked with a coy smile, her hair falling over one eye. "I like the sound of that."

EPILOGUE

OLIVIA SHIVERED and snuggled closer to Cole. He wrapped a well-muscled arm around her shoulder and pulled her in for a kiss, his peppermint coated lips moving hungrily over hers. She sucked on his bottom lip, the tension between them reaching a maddening pitch.

He'd been sampling her chapstick again.

It was a brisk morning, giving her the perfect excuse to cuddle up to her man and indulge in a little PDA. Not that she needed an excuse. Besides, she was having too much fun to care who was watching.

Five years in the city and she'd never even considered attending the Macy's Thanksgiving Day Parade. It had always seemed touristy, crowded, and freaking cold. But PBA had recently done some work for the retailer and Cole had scored passes to view the event from Harold Square. It was a once in a lifetime opportunity, and they were making the most of it, guzzling hot chocolate and reveling in the excitement with three million other happy parade goers.

"Having fun?" Cole asked, nipping at her frozen ear and warming it up with his steamy breath.

Desire stirred deep within her, desperate to be unleashed.

It was colder than a polar bear's butt and yet, somehow, he still managed to light a fire in her belly. He always had the effect, and it seemed to be growing stronger each day.

"With you? Always." And it was true. Over the last seven months she'd managed to find balance between work and life, opening herself to new experiences with Cole. With him, she was happier than she'd ever thought possible. "You know, I was thinking…"

"Oh?" he asked, lifting his mouth from her ear and looking her in the eye.

"Maybe we could duck out early and head back to your place to warm up before heading to White Plains." She arched her brow, letting him know *exactly* how she wanted to warm him up before dinner at his sister's house.

Lust flared in his eyes, softening the normally vibrant silver to a sensuous gray.

He spun her around so that her backside was pressed to the hard ridge of his erection, masking it from the crowd. His breath was hot on her cheek, sending a ripple of anticipation straight to her core. "You know, I like the way your mind works."

"Then you'll be really happy to know I'm not wearing any panties."

He groaned. "But we haven't even seen the man in the big red suit yet."

Kermit the Frog floated past with about fifty handlers dressed in green spandex.

Smiling, she leaned into Cole and circled her ass over his length. She cursed the twenty-five blocks separating them from his apartment. It might as well be on the moon for all the good it was doing them now. "I hate to be the bearer of bad news, but I'm pretty sure you're on the naughty list this year."

"Only one way to find out," he replied with a cocky grin. He smacked her bottom. "Besides, one look at you in those jeans and Santa's sure to understand."

"I wouldn't bet on it."

He reached inside her jacket and ran his finger along the waistband of her jeans, leaving a trail of fire in its wake. "I'm not the one running around town with no panties."

"Too bad."

They watched a few more musical acts before Santa finally made an appearance.

Led by his eight reindeer and riding in the trademark gold and emerald green sleigh, he arrived to the tune of "Santa Claus is Coming to Town." He waved cheerfully, shaking his belly and delighting the children, and apparently Cole, who grabbed her hand and pulled her from the edge of the crowd. Santa's float passed the landing zone in front of Macy's, a sure sign the three-hour parade was drawing to a close. The crowd clapped and cheered as the jolly old elf did something completely unexpected and descended from his float.

He scanned the crowd, his gaze landing on Olivia.

When he started walking toward her, she had a moment of panic.

Surely Cole wouldn't ask Santa about the naughty list, would he? Or about how good her ass looked in her skintight jeans? She was pretty sure he wouldn't mention the fact that she wasn't wearing underwear. Then again, she'd learned long ago not to underestimate him.

Oh, god. She was going to die of embarrassment.

Stealing a look at him, she saw he looked as surprised as she felt.

"Ho, ho, ho," Santa chortled, spreading his arms wide as if he meant to hug her. If she didn't know any better, she'd have thought he was the real deal with his rich velvet suit and snowy white beard. She tucked her hands in her pockets, resisting the urge to give his beard a tug Miracle on 34th Street style. "Merry Christmas, Olivia!"

How the hell did he know her name?

"Um. Hi, Santa." Because, yeah, what else could she say?

She glanced around, seeing a number of envious children staring at her.

Shouldn't he be talking to the kids? Getting their wish lists or and handing out candy canes? It had been a while since she'd sat on Santa's lap, but she was pretty sure things hadn't changed that much in the last twenty years.

"And what would you like for Christmas this year?" he asked, hooking his thumbs in the brown leather belt that wrapped around his massive mid-section. The bells on it tinkled, creating a melody that only Santa could pull off.

What did he expect her to ask for? Everything she needed was right next to her.

She glanced at Cole.

He shrugged, a mischievous grin lighting his face. No help there.

"Think you can manage world peace?" she asked, drawing on her pageant days.

You could never wrong with world peace.

"I'll see what I can do." He winked at her conspiratorially and reached into his pocket. "It's a bit early, but I have a very special gift for you today."

He pulled a small box out of his jacket. A robin egg blue box.

Tiffany blue, with a white satin bow, to be exact.

Olivia froze.

With gloved fingers, he pressed the tiny box into her hand. "Go ahead, dear. Open it."

Her eyes drifted to Cole, finding his gaze riveted on her.

Was this what she thought it was? Hope blossomed in her chest, her heart slamming against her rib cage double time. There was every possibility she was going to have a heart attack.

Surely not. It couldn't be. Could it?

With shaking hands, she pulled the bow loose, letting it drop to the ground and forgetting all about New York's strict littering laws. She flipped the box open, revealing the most stunning diamond ring she'd ever seen. Cushion cut, it was surrounded by a row of tiny diamonds that stretched down the band. It was totally classic and totally her.

Cole dropped to his knee, bringing tears to her eyes.

This was really happening. She couldn't believe it. Hadn't dared let herself imagine this day.

"Olivia, I love you more than life itself, and if you do me the honor of becoming my wife, I will spend every day for the rest of my life proving it to you. Will you marry me?"

Unable to suppress her emotions, tears of happiness leaked down her cheeks.

"Yes!" she cried, laughing through her tears and trying to commit the feeling to memory. Words couldn't describe the joy that was pouring from her heart. She was overwhelmed by it, knowing that she'd found her soul mate in Cole, knowing he'd be there with her each day for the rest of her life. Her equal, her partner. "Yes, yes, yes."

He leapt to his feet, swept her up in his arms, and crushed her to his solid chest. As he spun her around, the floats and the crowd dissolved into nothing more than a distant blur. Then and there, he claimed her as his own for all the world to see.

And secure in the knowledge Cole Bennett would be the last man she'd ever kiss, she crushed her lips to his, claiming him right back.

～

Thank you so much for reading Once Upon a Dare. Need more Risky Business in your life? Grab Chloe's story, Once Upon a Power Play!

ALSO BY JENNIFER BONDS

Waverly Wildcats

Holding Harper

Claiming Carter

Catching Quinn

Scoring Sutton

Protecting Piper

The Harts

Miles and Miles of You

Not Today, Cupid

Royally Engaged

A Royal Disaster

Royal Trouble

A Royal Mistake

The Risky Business Series

Once Upon a Dare

Once Upon a Power Play

Seducing the Fireman

ABOUT THE AUTHOR

Jennifer Bonds writes sizzling contemporary romance with sassy heroines, sexy heroes, and a whole lot of mischief. She's a sucker for enemies-to-lovers stories, laugh-out-loud banter, over-the-top grand gestures, and counts herself lucky to spend her days writing swoonworthy romance thanks to the support of amazing readers like you!

Jen lives in Pennsylvania, where her overactive imagination and weakness for reality TV keep life interesting. She's lucky enough to live with her own real-life hero, two adorable (and sometimes crazy) children, and one rambunctious K9. Loves Buffy, Mexican food, a solid Netflix binge, the Winchester brothers, cupcakes, and all things zombie. Sings off-key.

To connect with Jen, visit www.jenniferbonds.com to sign up for her newsletter and be the first to know about new releases, giveaways, and exclusive content! You can also find her on Facebook, Instagram, and TikTok @jbondswrites.